From Santa, With Love

SAMANTHA GAIL

DSTAR PUBLISHING LLC

CHAPTER 1
Hazel

"Okay, don't panic. Don't panic. We'll just pivot the plan." Hazel gripped the linoleum countertop so tightly that her knuckles turned white, which was a welcome reprieve from the reddish hue they typically sported all through the winter months in New York City. She stared down her reflection in the mirror hanging above the sink, reminding herself again. "Just. Pivot. The. Plan."

Who was she kidding? Her only serious relationship had gone up in smoke barely four months ago and now on her first real night of fun since then, she had spotted none other than her ex-boyfriend, Mike Downey, in the crowd by the food table. A Christmas party in Queens had sounded like a great way to distract herself from the nasty turn life had taken until she rounded the corner into the kitchen and caught her ex downing chips and salsa like a Hoover vacuum. Mike looked great, like he had lost some weight, and his hair had finally outgrown the shortly cropped hairstyle he preferred that Hazel had always secretly hated.

Well...maybe not *secretly*. She couldn't stop herself from telling Mike that her five year plan included a wedding with a man who had hair long enough to recreate the look from *27 Dresses*. After all, who wouldn't want to marry a dreamboat who looked like James Marsden? Mike had always laughed at her, as he often did when she mentioned her five year plan.

And then he dropped the bomb.

Mike didn't believe in marriage.

There hadn't been any trauma in his past. His parents were still happily married after almost forty years and both of his sisters were already married, each with the romantic, theatrical wedding of which Hazel aspired to emulate. Most of their friends were already married, or at least engaged, so it wasn't as though he had a horde of bachelors whispering in his ear. How could he not *believe* in marriage when he had only ever seen how fulfilling it could be?

The answer had been simple. He didn't believe in marriage *to her*. So Hazel had done the only respectable thing a 29 year old marketing executive could do. She broke up with him, moving all of her things into her cousin/best friend Blair's spare bedroom that smelled like burnt chocolate no matter how many candles she burned, and regrouped. Her five year plan required her to be married at 30, so she was cutting it down to the wire to find a suitable man for the job.

That's how Blair convinced her to come out tonight. A co-worker of Blair's invited everyone on their office floor to his townhome for a Christmas party, so Hazel was serving as Blair's plus one. An offer that sounded far more enticing when her ex-boyfriend was elsewhere in the city. He had never frequented Queens before! What was he doing here anyway?

But if there was one thing Hazel prided herself on, it was

how well she always managed to deviate when a curveball flew her way. It had been her mantra since grade school when she watched an episode of *Friends* and started formulating her five year plan.

"We'll just pivot the plan," she told her reflection firmly, a smile tugging at her lips. Life had already taught her that as long as she remained flexible in her methods, her goals were always accomplished. A Christmas party full of handsome strangers was the perfect opportunity to meet someone new who would cross off every requirement on her list for The Perfect Partner, thus keeping her plan in place.

Adjusting the headband with the small velvet top hat and holly she had donned in order to appear fun and festive, she fluffed her light brown waves and applied a fresh coat of her red tinted lip balm. She wouldn't let the sight of Mike Downey ruin her night. Her sparkly green mini dress complimented her curvy figure well, at least. It gave her the confidence she needed to leave the bathroom.

She stumbled in her clunky red heels as she stepped out into the hallway where a line of guests waited to use the facilities. A strong hand caught her by the elbow to steady her before she tumbled into the next person in line.

"Whoa there!" The hand extended from a tall man with dark tan skin, thick black hair that fell into his eyes, and a well-trimmed beard. He flashed her a bright smile, revealing pure white teeth, and nodded at her. It was easily the sexiest man Hazel had ever seen. "Had a bit too much to drink, have we?"

Hazel bristled at the insinuation. "I had exactly one Smirnoff cranberry out of the six pack, which is not enough for someone of my size to even have a buzz!" She would never allow herself to get drunk and lose control like that. Getting drunk led to wild, impulsive decisions, and those were definitely never part of The Plan.

Her savior grinned at her, making no effort to hide his perusal of her body. "Maybe we need to change that."

She rolled her eyes at his cockiness. "No, thanks, I've gotta find my cousin." Wrenching her arm from his grip, Hazel tottered down the hallway in the opposite direction from where she last saw Mike, cursing the too-tall heels Blair convinced her to wear. They might make her ass look "like a ripe peach" (Blair's words, not Hazel's), but they were ridiculous to walk in. Any self-respecting New Yorker should have known better.

Much to her chagrin, the man followed after her. "You're here with your cousin? Guy or girl?"

"Does it matter?" Hazel snapped. His enthusiasm irritated her and her nerves were already in overdrive from seeing her ex. She needed to find Blair and ask if she knew Mike was going to be here. Blair had never exactly been his biggest fan, so Hazel found it hard to believe she would have let Hazel come here knowing he would be there, too.

"Let me get you a drink," the mystery man offered. "It's a party, right?"

They emerged in a back den where the holiday music wasn't nearly as loud as the front living room/kitchen combo where most of the partygoers congregated. There were fewer people here, mostly engaged in casual conversation on the two couches, though some were leaning indifferently against the wall. A sliding glass door opened onto a minuscule concrete patio that let in enough cold air to counteract the heat from all the bodies packed into the townhouse. Real estate in New York never had much square footage, a fact that didn't stop the host from inviting what looked like a hundred people into his house. A white Christmas tree was wedged into the corner of the room, sporting enough twinkling lights to turn the room into a rave.

Blair, unfortunately, was nowhere to be seen. Hazel frowned, surveying the room again for the obnoxious sweater dress her cousin had worn along with her blue streaked hair, to no avail.

"I take it your cousin isn't here." The man's brown eyes twinkled merrily as he considered her disappointed slouch. "You should take me up on my offer for a drink."

"What is your problem? Do you always follow strangers around and insist they consume alcohol?" Hazel retorted.

His smile widened. "When they look as sexy as you, yeah. You look like the gift I want Santa to leave under my tree."

It was such a ridiculous pickup line that Hazel couldn't help but laugh. This man's arrogance knew no bounds! "Don't you even want to know my name? Or at least give me yours?"

He leaned into her, blocking one arm around her head as she backed into the door frame. She had to tilt her head up several inches to maintain eye contact. The intensity of his smolder made her gulp.

"My name is Alfie. Alfie Garza," he said. His eyes ran down the length of her body again, making her want to lean into him while simultaneously shielding herself from view.

Hazel blinked away at her rising lust. "I collect Care Bears," she responded, her voice an octave higher than was natural. "There are over 75 of them in my room. I can recite the entire Princess Diaries movie from memory because I've seen it so many times. My favorite food is baked pretzels, plain—no salt, even though I hate butter. Butter is so gross."

She hoped to turn him off with such absurd facts about her life and personality. A Casanova like this would definitely not meet any of the criteria on her Perfect Partner checklist. But Alfie just grinned and let his elbow bend so that his chest barely brushed hers. "I like Care Bears."

His smug face was getting closer and closer, sending Hazel into a whirlwind of panic. "This is not how to pick up a woman..." she murmured, focusing on his lush lips that looked like they were headed straight for her. It didn't matter that he smelled like divinely expensive cologne or that he knew enough to coordinate his belt with his shoes. It also didn't matter that he was one of the most gorgeous men she had ever seen, with brown eyes that held a myriad of hues, all set on her.

Kissing a strange man she didn't know at a Christmas party was not part of The Plan. Sure, he was handsome, but she—Hazel McAllister—did not kiss random men. Her kissing partners included one stint of Seven Minutes in Heaven her senior year of high school and a few spontaneous make out partners from dares at the sorority house in college. That was all before she met Mike, though. Mike, who was supposed to be The Perfect Partner, changed everything, then changed it all back in a single night.

Alfie's lips were about to collide with hers and Hazel couldn't remember if she used the good toothpaste that kept her breath fresh longer or the whitening toothpaste that gave her a brighter smile. What if the supermodel of a man kissed her and she left a bad taste in his mouth? What if she had forgotten the proper etiquette to kissing with tongue? It was all happening too fast, time moving in a blur like a roller coaster barreling down the first hill, and—

"Hazel?!" Blair called out in alarm.

CHAPTER 2
Blair

Her eyes had to be playing tricks on her. Maybe her drink was drugged. There was no way her cousin and bestie for the resties, Hazel "Always Uptight" McAllister, would be caught dead in a darkened doorway getting cozy with a handsome stranger.

Okay, so it wasn't exactly dark in a room full of twinkling Christmas lights. And okay, so nothing had actually happened yet. But the tension crackled the air between them with a surge of sexual electricity that even Blair could feel. She had been looking everywhere for Hazel ever since she spotted her ex and had no idea how Hazel managed to run from one man just to wind up panting after another.

She loved a good meet cute just as well as the next Gen Z'er, but at some point, you had to have a level head and recognize it could go from zero to psycho in a millisecond. Her BFF was not the kind of person who believed life could operate like a Kate Hudson romcom, so it was entirely likely that this was an unwanted intrusion that Hazel couldn't navigate her way out of.

"Hazel?!" Blair cried in alarm. She held her arms out wide,

blocking the narrow hallway. One hand held a Solo cup of some sort of tequila mixer that Blair had already downed in full before refilling it to the brim in the kitchen. The night was going to be a disaster no matter what after she told her cousin her big news, so Blair decided to let loose early into the night.

All of that was going to be derailed, however, if she had to stop Hazel from doing something she would regret.

"Um, excuse me!" Blair karate chopped on the man's elbow, forcing him to pull his arm away from her cousin and back away a couple steps. She flashed Hazel a look that was equal parts are-you-alright/do-you-want-me-to-kill-him. Hazel, however, looked awestruck and didn't seem to mind that some handsome, hulking stranger had almost kissed her.

"Everything's fine," Hazel assured her while keeping her eyes on the man. "Alfie and I were just saying our goodbyes."

Blair snorted and glanced at the man skeptically. "'Alfie?' In all the fake names of the world, you chose 'Alfie?'"

The man gave her an easygoing grin. "It's not a fake name. Alfie Garza, at your service." He held out a hand to shake.

She rounded on her cousin instead, not making any attempts to keep her voice down. "What has gotten into you?!"

To her surprise, Hazel looked back at Alfie and smiled. "We were just discussing the appropriate way to approach a lady. That's all."

Alfie had the good grace to smile sheepishly at Hazel, rubbing a hand through his thick waves of black hair. His button down shirt was so tailored to his body that it moved like a second skin and Blair had to bite back a cheer.

GET IT, Hazel! If her cousin was finally going to act like a normal person and hook up at a party, she could do a lot worse than tall, dark, and handsome.

The music in the front of the townhouse transitioned to the next holiday song, sending several partygoers in the back den into a frenzy of whoops and hollers. A few of them left the room in a craze towards the dancing area in the front living room, and in so doing, created a slo-mo montage for the ages in Blair's mind. One of the guests knocked into Alfie, who was still blocking the doorway. He practically dove face first into Hazel's substantial cleavage while his arm went flying in an attempt to catch himself and collided with the Solo cup in Blair's hand that unfortunately contained a bright red concoction of juice and tequila. A bright red concoction that was now dousing Blair from head to toe in her snow white Christmas sweater dress.

She was mortified. It was her co-worker's party and she had already seen her boss lurking around in the kitchen. Blair had not yet told them about her big news either, though she expected them to have the same reaction as Hazel, with just enough courtesy to express said reaction behind closed doors. This was NOT the last impression she wanted to give them before she returned to work on Monday and made her announcement.

"What the *fuck?*" she sputtered, trying to wipe the burning alcohol from her eyes.

"Oh, man, I'm so sorry!" Alfie yelled. "Hey, bro, you're a fucking dickhead!"

Blair had to assume his last sentiment was directed towards the guest who plowed into them and not her, but that was purely an assumption at that point because she was too busy blinking away the tequila that was now setting her eyeballs on fire.

"Here, let me help you!" Hazel crooned. Soft hands grabbed onto hers and turned her back towards the kitchen, but Blair put a hand on the wall to halt their movement.

"I will take care of this. You stay and take care of Prince Charming."

"Are you sure?" Hazel whispered in concern.

"Unless you need an out, yes, I am entirely sure that I don't want my bestie cleaning me up." Blair knew her attitude was unfair because none of this was Hazel's fault, but she wanted to regain some of her dignity before anyone from the office saw her. They already viewed her as semi-incompetent, and needing someone else to clean her up after a mishap at a party was not the way to improve that reputation.

She managed to bring enough into focus that she could make out the blurry lines of other people and determine doorways. Dustin, the work associate hosting the party, had told her that he kept a box of forgotten things in the townhome's sole storage closet from all the parties he hosted. Dustin was apparently a wannabe DJ on the weekends and hosted ragers every Friday and Saturday night. While it might be repulsive to put on a stranger's dirty cast offs, at least Blair would be the one solving the problem instead of someone else finding the solution for her. That's what adults did.

Or so she had been told.

Now if she could just remember where the closet was, life would be kosher. As she wove in and out of people milling in the hallway, averting her eyes from their quizzical stares, Blair found a closed door on the right hand side just before the hallway opened into the kitchen/living room combo. That had to be it! And not a minute too soon, she realized, as her boss, a perpetually crabby man with a Tom Selleck mustache, emerged from the kitchen area with a plate full of Christmas cookies in hand.

She yanked open the door, momentarily surprised at how heavy it was, and dashed inside, praying her boss hadn't seen her latest catastrophe. A pale light bulb hung from the ceiling, already illuminating the small space, and she felt a thrill of triumph when she recognized the blurry lines of shelves.

The door had only just swung shut with a heavy thud behind her when a man stepped forward from the depths of the closet and cried out, "No! Don't let it close!"

Did this party have a gravitational pull for freaks? Was it normal for Dustin to allow men to hide out in dark corners and lunge at the first woman who crossed their path? First the hulking hunk turning Hazel into a flirt and now an axe murderer stalking his prey in the throng of people. Blair didn't want to go out like Chanel #2 from *Scream Queens*.

Wait a second, she recognized that voice...

"Mike?!" she asked incredulously.

CHAPTER 3

Mike

The odds of winding up at a Christmas party in Queens with his ex-girlfriend were already so low that Mike was struggling to compute the math, but now adding in the possibility that he would get locked in a closet with said ex-girlfriend's cousin was almost an astronomical improbability. Whoever ruled the Universe at the moment must be having a laugh at his expense because there was no way this was happening. He wasn't even supposed to be at this party!

"Yeah, Blair, it's me," Mike admitted with a sigh. "You just locked us in here."

"WHAT?" she screeched. She turned around only to discover what Mike had discovered approximately 25 minutes ago—there was no door handle on the inside of the closet. They were stuck.

Blair pounded on the door, wailing for someone to come help her, blue streaked curls bouncing with every bang. She looked like a Christmas Wonderland on crack in a white sweater dress with large plastic snowflakes hanging every few centimeters. The dress made a clacking sound from all of her movements.

"Nobody can hear you!" He finally barked after allowing her a minute to panic. He sank back into his earlier seat of a stray cushion on the floor.

She turned back to him with wide eyes and he realized the front of her body was covered in red stains. Her hair was wet around her face, making some of the white sparkles drip from her eye shadow.

"You mean I'm stuck in here with you?!" she crowed in a high voice. "No, no, NO!" Blair resumed pounding on the door and tried unsuccessfully to shove it open.

Mike sighed. He was already sporting a decent headache from eating real food for the first time in a couple days. Adding her frantic beating to the mix did nothing to alleviate the pain in his temple.

"Someone will find us eventually. Or they'll turn the music down," he tried to console her.

Blair turned back to him, tears streaking down her cheeks. "But that could be hours!"

"I don't suppose you have your cell phone on you," he suggested.

Her hip jutted out, a fist resting top. "Does it look like this dress has pockets for a phone?"

He merely shook his head. It was better to spend his time formulating a reasonable story to give the townhome's owner as to why Mike was locked inside the closet during a Christmas party to which he was not invited. Besides, he knew how dramatic Blair could be, and saying anything else to her at that moment would likely set her in a tailspin. Blair and Hazel were alike in that way.

She brushed the tears from her cheeks and started looking around the small space. Floor to ceiling shelves were crammed in an L shape in the stainless steel room. It had a very industrial air that looked out of place with the rest of the home that Mike had seen. Most of the shelves were full of plastic totes or cardboard boxes, but in his initial inspection, all he found were old photographs, an air fryer, and some Halloween decorations. Nothing that would be remotely useful in getting them out.

Blair, however, had not yet arrived at that conclusion and began haphazardly throwing things out of boxes.

"Hey!" Mike barked when a pink cowboy boot narrowly missed his face.

She let out an exasperated tut. "Don't you want to get out of here?"

"Yeah, but I'm not going to ruin some poor guy's closet in my attempt to do so!"

Blair rolled her eyes. "Dustin would hardly care. He told me this is mostly junk left over from the parties he throws on the weekends." She suddenly turned to him, suspicion marring her features. "Do you *know* Dustin...?"

Mike swallowed hard, debating whether or not to tell her the truth. She clearly knew the owner and would most likely tell Hazel if they ever got out of this place. The truth wasn't something he was ready for Hazel to learn.

"Sure. Yeah, I met him a while back," Mike lied.

His companion was too determined in her search to care. "There's got to be something in here!" she burst out in frustration. "Who has a closet without a doorknob?"

Mike had wondered the exact same thing, but he was hardly in a position to judge. "You might as well get comfortable. We might be here for a while." He pulled his knees up to prop his elbows on and leaned his head back against the metal shelf behind him.

Blair sighed in defeat and nodded glumly. "I came in here to try and find a change of clothes. I had a little accident with my drink." She waved at the front of her dress, the crimson stain shifting as the snowflakes moved, then turned back to a dilapidated brown box with articles of clothing hanging out. Holding up a faded black concert tee, she asked, "Think this will work?"

He shrugged. She was pretty petite and the shirt looked enormous. "It's just me, anyways. No one to impress in here."

Nodding, Blair pulled her white combat boots off. Mike couldn't think of anyone else who styled things like Blair McAllister, but somehow it always worked for her. No one would think to pair those with a Christmas sweater dress and fishnet stockings in a tie-dyed red and green pattern, yet she pulled it off with flair. Her rich brown skin had a glimmering sheen to it, even under the pale light, along with her corkscrew brown and blue curls, and Mike couldn't help but smile. She embodied the creative boho style.

"Don't peek!" she instructed, turning away from him to yank the destroyed dress over her head.

It wasn't intentional, but when Mike tried to turn his body in the opposite angle, his hand slipped on the cold steel floor and his eyes darted upward as he momentarily fell, his eyes landing briefly on the lacy white panties she wore. He instantly averted his gaze back down, willing his brain to erase the image from his memory. Mike had always thought Blair was attractive in an artistic type of way, but seeing the smooth arch of her back and the round curves of her ass made him want to do a double take.

That's your ex's cousin, asshole! he chided himself.

"So how do you know Dustin?" Mike asked to distract himself from the direction his thoughts were taking.

She huffed, tugging the shirt down in a vain attempt for it to hit mid-thigh. The shoulders and collar of the shirt were stretched, making it hang awkwardly off one shoulder. "We work together," Blair ground out. She sank onto the ground across from him, angling her legs forward and crossing them at the ankles.

Mike nodded. Unless she had changed jobs since he and Hazel broke up, Blair was a graphic designer at a software company. Of course the statistics worked against him and the random party he found was hosted by Blair's co-worker. That seemed to be the way his luck went lately.

Silence descended as they both tried to figure out what to say. Echoes of laughter and shouts filtered through the door, barely audible above the sounds of *Rockin' Around the Christmas Tree*. Blair adjusted her arms so her hands were under her thighs and shivered slightly.

Without a second thought, Mike shrugged out of his cardigan, a birthday gift from Hazel shortly before they broke up, and handed it to her. Her amber eyes flashed at him in irritation before sighing and slipping her arms through the sleeves. He realized her legs were still in the fishnets and must be even colder on the metal floor. Standing up, Mike leaned over her head to open a plastic tote he had searched in earlier and found unused holiday tablecloths. Snatching the one on top with a Rudolph so faded that his nose was gone, Mike crouched down next to her.

"Lift up your legs," he ordered.

Blair's eyes widened, but she held up her legs as instructed. He tried to be quick about it, leaving the tablecloth folded in half as he slid it under her calves. The angle gave him an unobstructed view of her thighs, muscular from the hip hop dancing team she still participated in, and he forced himself to picture his great-grandmother's face when he felt his cheeks heat.

He sat back down across from her, ignoring the way her eyes burned into the top of his head that now hung in shame. It was wrong for him to be lusting after his ex-girlfriend's cousin, someone who had never hidden the fact she didn't particularly care for him. Even though he knew the breakup with Hazel was the right thing to do, he would never want to hurt her by doing anything with Blair. She was purely off limits.

"So why don't we discuss how you broke Hazel's heart?" Blair suddenly asked.

Mike snorted. "Most people just thank someone when they're considerate."

"Thank you." Blair's voice was curt. "But I still want to know why you did my cousin dirty."

His sigh was heavy as he processed the right way to explain it. Blair was loyal to her cousin, who had really been raised more like a sister to her, and although he was no longer with Hazel, Mike still respected the hell out of her and missed certain parts of their relationship.

"It's hard to disappoint the one you love," he finally replied. "It's even harder to realize the person you're disappointing isn't actually someone who loves you back. And if you'll remember, she's the one who broke up with me."

She snorted derisively. "You're trying to tell me you think Hazel didn't love you?"

"When did she ever express love for me outside of her checklist?" Mike challenged, his gray eyes fierce. "It was never about me, Blair, it was about the life Hazel was determined to make for herself."

Blair considered this for a moment before nodding. "There's nothing wrong with going after what you want," she offered lamely.

Mike nodded in agreement. "No, there isn't," he said, "but I couldn't let myself watch her start to resent me because I couldn't be the person she wanted."

CHAPTER 4

Alfie

If Heaven was anything other than falling face first into Hazel's breasts, Alfie wanted no part of it. As embarrassing as the moment was, he wanted to permanently plant his face there and give them the attention they deserved. Hazel had caught his eye the moment he spotted her at his next door neighbor's Christmas party, and when the opportunity presented itself to follow her to the bathroom after she ran out of the kitchen like her skirt was on fire, he took it. Alfie was nothing if not an opportunist.

Now, though, he needed to do some damage control because the look on Hazel's face indicated she was a second away from going into nuclear orbit. Her face had gone red and her lips were puckering. If she started crying, he would panic because he had dealt with enough crying women in the past few weeks to last a lifetime.

Unsure of what else to do, he pulled her closer and tucked her head under his chin. "It's all good," he assured her, rubbing her back in slow strokes. "It was just an accident."

"This whole night has been an accident!" she burst out.

Darting from his arms, she tore off down the hallway, pushing others out of the way and tottering on those damned heels of hers.

He paused for a moment before taking off after her. She stopped long enough to grab her coat and purse from the pile on the stairs before racing out into the night. It was cold outside, snow and ice coating every surface, and Alfie had a mental image of her splayed out on the sidewalk after slipping in her sparkly red shoes. It hit too close to home after everything with his sister and he found himself chasing her down outside.

"Let me make sure you get home safely," Alfie panted when he reached her. "You shouldn't be out in this wearing those." He gestured towards her feet.

She shook her head angrily. "Aren't you taking this a little too far just to get laid? There are plenty of other women inside!"

It was cute when she was mad. Hazel couldn't have been more than 5'2 without her heels on, which made him feel like a giant standing over a dwarf at his 6'4. With the holiday lights all around, her porcelain skin reflected the bright lights, making him think of a Christmas angel. She glared up at him and placed her fists on her hips, ready for a fight.

Alfie smiled at her instead of rising to meet her anger. "I'm too busy shootin' my shot with you."

Letting out a groan of irritation, Hazel turned away from him and started pulling something out of the large tote bag serving as a purse on her shoulder. He watched in fascination as she pulled out tall snow boots with fur lining the top. Balancing on one leg, she yanked a glittery heel off and threw it on the ground, shoving her foot into the boot with an angry thrust.

He bent down and picked up the discarded shoe, holding his

free hand out for the second one after she repeated the exercise for the other foot.

"Thank you," Hazel said begrudgingly, taking Dorothy's knockoffs from him and tossing them in her bag.

Alfie crossed his arms over his chest as the wind whipped around them. A newly arriving guest catcalled someone as they clambered up the short set of stairs into the townhome where the party was still in full swing.

"Now where?" asked Alfie. He rubbed his hands up and down his arms for warmth. Since the party was just next door, he hadn't bothered to wear a winter coat.

Hazel ignored him, pulling out her cell phone and typing a message in loud pecks. Before she could stop him, Alfie snatched the phone from her grip to program his number into it, then handed it back with a broad smile.

"Now that I know you can always reach me," he teased, "where to?"

She rolled her eyes. "I am going home to pivot this night into something enjoyable."

Alfie made a show of turning around to look on the sidewalk around them. "Is there a couch we're moving?"

Hazel blinked at him, the look on her face making it clear that she questioned his sanity. "I beg your pardon?"

He shrugged. "Only Ross Geller uses words like 'pivot.'"

Despite her annoyance, she laughed. It eased some of the tension from her shoulders and made her body relax. "He has a great vocabulary."

"Never pegged you for liking a show as bad as that one," Alfie commented, twisting his lips in skepticism.

It was another one of her triggers because Hazel immediately fired off again. "*Friends* was one of the top rated shows of its time and still has new generations of fans forming every day! It is the quintessential sitcom!"

He shrugged a shoulder and started to walk away from her towards the steps to his own townhouse. "Adolf Hitler used to be popular, too, and we all saw how that turned out." He hoped teasing her would keep her attention because he liked the flush that crept up her neck when she got angry. There was something about Hazel that captivated his attention and he wasn't ready for the night to end with her. It was unlikely that she would keep his number at this point, though.

Alfie was immediately rewarded as she sputtered out, "Oh my god! You did not just compare a fascist dictator to my favorite tv show!" The sounds of heavy footfalls followed him, but stopped abruptly as he reached his door.

"Where are you going?" she huffed. Her hands were balled into fists on her hips again.

Alfie inclined his head towards his front door. "Inside to get a coat. It's too cold out here without one. Unless you'd rather just come inside and continue the debate." His grin only served to rile her up more.

"I already told you, I will not be your one night stand!" She all but stomped in her frustration. "I've never done that in my life," Hazel added, almost in afterthought.

Alfie's gaze softened somewhat at her disclosure. "Good thing I haven't either," he admitted. When her eyes dashed to his face, hopeful and sincere, he couldn't help but add, "Although maybe we can pop each other's cherries!"

She rolled her eyes and crossed her arms across her chest. "It *wasn't* nice meeting you, Alfie." Adjusting the bag on her shoulder, she turned left to leave.

His window of opportunity was closing and while a voice in

his head questioned why he cared so much, Alfie didn't want Hazel to leave. There was something about her that reminded him of his sister Rita, and wasn't that the whole reason he agreed to go to his neighbor's party in the first place? To be around someone—anyone—who would help him feel better about celebrating the holidays after such a devastating loss?

"If you've got something more comfortable to wear in that giant backpack, you're welcome to come in and change," Alfie offered. "I'll stay outside here, scout's honor." He held up three fingers and crossed the other hand over his heart.

She chewed at her bottom lip, contemplating the decision. The cold worked in his favor, a frigid wind blowing down the road, forcing her to hug her coat tighter around her body. "It's not a backpack," Hazel corrected him as she finally climbed the steps up to him. "And I only have a spare pair of leggings, but at least then my legs won't be cold."

He nodded as though it was perfectly normal for a woman to carry around a small suitcase filled with spare clothing. Maybe that was a part of the Girl Code his sister never taught him.

"You're welcome to any of my hoodies." He held up his hands in a peaceful gesture.

She swept past him, entering through the front door Alfie had just unlocked and paused in the foyer. "This is your place?" Hazel asked, her voice small.

Alfie stepped into the doorway just enough to reach the hook by the door that held his heavy wool coat. "For the past two years," he replied.

"It's beautiful." Her words caught in her throat as she surveyed her surroundings.

Alfie's mother had spent a fortune hiring an interior decorator who would bring in elements of his Spanish heritage, creating a warm ambiance of browns and reds. A tiled mosaic of the Alhambra palace hung on the wall above the white sofa while two brown leather armchairs sat opposite. An arched frame opened into the kitchen, smaller than Dustin's next door, after Alfie had a contractor remove the dining area to accommodate the Spanish Renaissance style piano in the back corner. Large cream floor candles were spread throughout the room, their smaller counterparts lining every flat surface available.

He shrugged nonchalantly. "Helps remind me of home."

"Home?" Hazel turned to look back at him, arching a curved brow in question.

Alfie nodded. "Spain. I grew up in a metropolitan barrio of Madrid."

The surprise was evident on her face. "But you don't have an accent."

It would have been simple to throw out the name of his famous parents and show off his wealthy upbringing as he had with countless other women in the past, but something held Alfie back. Maybe it was the way her eyes were bright with curiosity like Rita's always were, or maybe it was simply the fact that it was the first time all night she was showing real interest in him. It wasn't worth losing the little bit of ground he had established with her to start bragging about his parents' success as *the* leading actress and most award winning composer in Spanish cinema.

"I spent a lot of time in the United States for school," he settled on. It sounded plausible, at least.

The answer satisfied her enough that she turned away from him and peered up his stairs.

"It's just us," Alfie said with a smile.

"You live alone?" Hazel inquired, the surprise even more apparent in her tone.

He grinned cheekily at her. "Until I convince you to stay."

This time she merely laughed at him. "Did you mean it when you said I can borrow a sweatshirt?"

"Of course." Alfie took a step further into the room and pointed up the stairs. "My bedroom is on the right. Help yourself to anything."

She blinked at him with her mouth open. "You're not going up with me?"

As much as the thought excited him, Alfie could tell that she was on the edge of bolting. This was not a woman accustomed to being around strangers, nor was she entirely ready to trust him yet. Since he had nothing to hide, he shook his head and waved her forward like a gameshow host. "*Eres bienvenido a cualquier cosa*," he replied. *You are welcome to do anything.*

Hazel gave him a tight smile. "*Qué anfitrión hospitalario.*" *What a hospitable host.*

She sauntered up the stairs, her wide hips swaying like a vixen.

If the sight of her ascending the stairs wasn't enough to send blood rushing to his dick, hearing her respond in flawless Spanish made him readjust his pants. Perhaps Hazel was the Christmas miracle he needed to get his mind off the train wreck his life had become.

"Thank you, Santa," he whispered.

CHAPTER 5

Hazel

She hoped Blair saw her text message right away and didn't panic when she couldn't find Hazel anywhere at the party. It was all just too much. Seeing Mike reminded Hazel of how much she failed. Relationships were something she had always pushed to the side in favor of racking up more accomplishments, and she was not taking the disappointment well.

Valedictorian at her high school? Done.

Graduating summa cum laude in marketing from the University of Pennsylvania? Child's play.

Becoming the youngest marketing executive ever at Norwell Technology, Inc.? Completed before her 27th birthday.

Hazel was a pro at crossing goals off her checklist in every other aspect of her life, but it was either naiveté or arrogance that led her to assume romantic relationships would be just as simple.

Mike really seemed like The Perfect Partner. He had a great job as a data analyst with USA Today, he came from a good family, and they had a lot of mutual friends. Their lives were busy—fulfilling—and to Hazel, it was like her whole life fell into place. She had been looking at houses in the highest rated school districts in Connecticut and New Jersey, expecting a proposal to come at any moment. It never occurred to her that they both weren't working towards the same five year plan.

So why was she acting so out of character now? Yes, Alfie may have missed his calling as a supermodel, but that didn't mean she should root through his closet and wear one of his hoodies. Although he claimed he wasn't into one night stands, his flirtatious commentary suggested that he was open to the possibility. Why would Hazel entertain that? This wasn't one of Blair's cheesy romcoms. Hazel wouldn't give up her entire five year plan and all her hard work just because of one lousy Christmas party, even if Alfie had descended from Mount Olympus.

The only conclusion Hazel could draw was that she was lonely. She was used to having someone to text or call, someone to spend her weekends and evenings with to talk about her day. Their friend group had primarily taken her side, appalled that Mike would behave so rashly, but she couldn't stand always being the lone ranger in a sea of couples. Dodging their phone calls and creating excuses to refuse their invitations had become second nature.

Alfie didn't know her as the Hazel with Mike, however, and that was incredibly alluring. It was almost like she had a blank slate without the guilt of her relationship failure looming over her head.

His bedroom closet held mostly tailored suits and button downs, but in the very back she found a worn hoodie with Real Madrid Futbol written across the front. She knew he had been surprised when she responded in Spanish, which was the reaction most people had when they realized she was bilingual. In today's economic market, it had been a skillset that just made sense. However, it was equally as shocking to learn he was originally from Spain. There wasn't a single hint of accent. Would he have taken the time to work with a dialect coach like she did?

Throwing his hoodie over her head, she wiggled out of her dress by dragging it down her legs and then pulled the leggings up. Thankfully she wore a thong and wouldn't have panty lines. Not that anyone could see them in Alfie's sweatshirt that fell just above her knees.

Since she was already dressed far more casually than normal, she decided to really get comfortable and used a makeup remover wipe from her purse to take off the heavy eyeshadow Blair had applied for the party. It made her face look more like her usual self, improving her mood. The full length mirror on the back of his door confirmed she looked normal, albeit in clothing a few sizes too big.

She descended the stairs to join Alfie in the foyer and tried to hide the blush creeping up her neck at his wicked smile. He arched an eyebrow, the tip of his tongue poking out between his teeth as he gave her body the same perusal as before.

"I could get used to the sight of you in my shirt," he commented playfully.

Hazel smiled back at him, suddenly shy and apprehensive. "Thank you for letting me borrow your hoodie. I promise I'll wash it and return it."

"Sounds to me like we have a second date booked, then."

She rolled her eyes and started shrugging her coat on. "Slow down, hotrod. We haven't had a first date." Her light brown hair cascaded down around her shoulders as she pulled the hood out from under the collar of her coat before he tugged on the open seam to bring her closer.

"What do you think this is, *aguerrida?*" he murmured. He slowly pulled the zipper of her coat upward, letting his fingers lightly trail along the center of her body. The dark brown hues of his eyes captivated her, and she unintentionally gulped as she clenched her thighs together.

It took her brain an extra moment to translate what he said because he was so damned yummy!

"Hey—I'm not feisty!" she argued. She took a giant step backward as if to emphasize her point. "And this isn't a date!"

Alfie smirked, but didn't contradict her. Withdrawing a scarf from a basket near the door, he wound it around her neck, leaving it loose enough that she could adjust it, if need be. He reached into the pocket of her coat and withdrew her gloves, then waited for her to put them on so he could wind his fingers through hers.

Part of her wanted to fight him on principle while the other part reminded her that she was choosing the blank slate. She could be the Hazel she was before Mike, even if it was hard to remember who exactly that was.

With that thought in mind, she allowed him to lead her out into the cold winter night.

They walked in companionable silence for a few blocks. Her hand remained warmly ensconced in his, but Hazel argued against the voice in her head that it was for safety purposes. Some areas of the sidewalk were really slick! Once it became clear that he was heading towards the subway, however, it was time for her to dig in her heels.

"You cannot be serious right now!" she cried. "I am NOT getting on the train!"

Alfie grinned. "Are you scared or something?"

Hazel rolled her eyes again. "Can you be a grown up for two

seconds? Respectable people do not ride on the train from Flushing at—" She whipped out her phone to glance at the clock, "—eleven thirty-four at night!"

He contemplated for a minute before weaving his other hand around her face to cup her cheek. Staring deeply into her eyes, he quietly asked, "Do you know how to trust anybody or is it just me?"

"Oh, no! You don't get to psychoanalyze me! I'm allowed to dislike something, Alfie."

"Fine," he amended. "We can call an Uber, but you have to agree to go anywhere I want tonight."

She couldn't believe her ears. The nerve of this man! "I can call my own Uber. I can go anywhere I want. I can—"

"Yeah, yeah. We all know you're Miss Independent, *aguerrida*, but I'm asking you to let me make this night special for both of us." There was a pleading note to his voice that made her pause long enough to take a deep breath. He was asking her to pivot. Didn't she do that every day anyway? That was what made her different than those stupid romance movies. She wasn't so set in her ways that she couldn't see the forest through the trees.

On the exhale, Hazel settled her shoulders and nodded. "Okay. Fine. Wherever you want to go."

His resulting smile sent a flashing wake up call straight to her vagina because she was suddenly highly alert to the way her body yearned for his. "Then let's go have some Christmas fun."

CHAPTER 6

Blair

This definitely wasn't how she foresaw the night going, but truth be told, being locked inside a cold, metal closet with Mike Downey was a right side better than what her alternative had been. She knew that Hazel only wanted what was best for her, except the only thing that was "best" just so happened to always be whatever Hazel wanted. Since Hazel was like the older sister she never had, Blair didn't know how to stand up to her, and the thought of doing so right before Christmas was enough to make her stress eat. That was why she made a beeline for the party food the second they walked through the door, which was obviously the reason Hazel found Mike there in the first place!

She had learned how to always place the blame on her shoulders at the tender age of 5 when, awestruck by Hazel's much older, confident persona, she had allowed Hazel to cut their hair. Blair would be the practice dummy, Hazel had decided, and so she would cut Blair's hair first in order to perfect the act. Dramatic pixie cuts were all the rage, which meant they could both start school the next month in style. Except Hazel had butchered her hair to the point where it was barely visible on parts of her head, and when Blair's mother came in the room and discovered them, Blair insisted the whole thing had been her idea because she didn't want to risk losing Hazel's favor.

And so went their relationship for the rest of their lives. While she had grown a backbone—to some degree—for the most part, Hazel still called the shots. It was Hazel who encouraged her to turn her interest in art into graphic design because "graphic design is such a marketable skill" rather than focusing on painting like she'd wanted. But she had been right; Blair didn't struggle to find a job after graduation. And when Hazel suggested it was time for her to get her own apartment because real estate was "such a worthy investment," she had dropped a huge chunk of savings into the down payment on a place that Hazel liked because of its close proximity to restaurants and shopping, even though it was a good ways out from the museums Blair liked to frequent in her spare time. It had been a worthy investment in some regard, though, because less than eight months later, she had Hazel as a roommate when that prick dashed her hopes and spit on her dreams.

A prick who was now trapped in the metal box with her, looking tired and forlorn. Mike had always been a good looking guy. Maybe not leading man quality, but still decent enough that you could take photos with him at any given moment and not stress about uploading them on socials. But now his skin was looking a little gray and his hair was in desperate need of a cut. Initially it looked like he had lost weight, but in the dismal light of the closet, the weight loss was more apparent and extreme.

Blair had wanted to yell at him and insult him to her heart's content. Knowing Mike, he would have let her because he was a silent and stoic kind of guy. Hardly ever rattled. But his explanation of their breakup pulled at Blair's heartstrings a little bit and reined in her commentary.

Sheer boredom made her want to pepper him with questions at the moment. His eyes had remained closed for the past half hour, though, and she didn't want to wake him if he was asleep. When his wristwatch indicated an hour had passed, however, she hit her breaking point.

"So why are you really here?" Blair asked. She had resorted to doing dance stretches on the floor to keep her blood flowing, resulting in the front split position she currently held.

Mike blinked his eyes open and turned to her. It was the only indication that he hadn't actually been sleeping, but his eyes widened before averting his gaze to the floor at the sight of her legs. She resumed a cross legged position and tucked a second tablecloth over her lap, waiting expectantly for his answer.

He shrugged before letting out a small chuckle. The chuckle grew to an outright laugh that escalated to borderline hysterics where he clutched his side and the boom of his laughter echoed off the steel walls. A tear actually ran down the side of his face as he leaned over.

Was this the point of her Lifetime movie where everyone realized who the killer was? Would Blair wind up stuffed into one of the plastic totes for her body to decompose, only to be found weeks later? Mike had never fit the stereotype of a serial killer, but that didn't always mean anything.

Stop it! The good angel on her right was snapping at the wicked devil on her left. *This is Mike Downey, for fuck's sake!*

Sometimes Blair questioned why she always envisioned a Tom and Jerry style cartoon setup for her conscious self, but then she remembered that lots of people married their prison pen pals, so who was she to question such a minor life choice?

"Okay, I'm missing the joke," she told him after the din finally lowered.

Mike sat up straighter, wiping the last lingering tears on his cheeks, before propping his elbows on his upright knees again. "Can you keep a secret?" he asked, a chuckle still lingering in his voice.

"Secret" could only be code for "don't tell Hazel," and while Blair knew it was unlikely that she would manage to keep her mouth shut, she was also really curious as to what Mike could possibly want to keep from her cousin. She only paused for a moment before nodding in the affirmative. It was Mike's fault if he couldn't remember that Blair tended to fold like a cheap suit whenever private information was brought up.

"I couldn't turn down the chance for free food," he finally admitted. He glanced quickly at her face before focusing on the shelf in front of him. "It's the first time I've eaten anything substantial in a few days."

Blair blinked in confusion. While Mike had always been frugal, he was never that uptight about his budget that he didn't buy groceries. "Data analysts at your level aren't that poor, Mike. You can find some other way to save money."

He tried to smile but it came off as more of a grimace. "I'm not a data analyst anymore."

Say what now? This was news to Blair because Mike had been very close to a promotion when he and Hazel were last together. He was the most wholesome, by the rules kind of guy she had ever met—perfect for someone with plans and checklists like her cousin—so what could he have possibly done that was bad enough to warrant being fired?

"I'm pretty sure you qualify for unemployment of some kind," Blair offered in a vain attempt to be helpful. "You were at that company for almost eleven years, Mike."

Mike shook his head sadly. "They don't offer unemployment when you voluntarily leave," he explained.

Blair blinked in surprise. "Why would you voluntarily leave a job when you were about to be promoted?" That was very un-Mike like.

He sighed and stood up in a stretch. After turning away from her for a moment, he turned his head over his shoulder and admitted, "I left because when they offered me the promotion, I realized I never wanted to be a data analyst. And the thought of spending one more second sequestered behind a desk crunching numbers made me want to throw up."

That was the last thing Blair could ever imagine Mike saying. In that final sentence he had perfectly summarized her entire life's problem. They had never had anything in common like that before, however, and it was like hearing a note sung off key to realize she and Mike were sharing the same experience.

After a hesitant moment, she asked, "Well what do you want to do?"

Mike turned back to face her and leaned against the shelf behind him. He stared at the ceiling as he remarked, "I always wanted to write a science fiction novel, like Isaac Asimov."

An inconsistent career like that would have definitely been an issue for Hazel, Blair realized. It was quite the revelation, because although she knew Mike enjoyed reading and had a bookshelf full of tattered paperbacks, she could not remember a single time he voiced such aspirations in front of her. As she studied him in the pale gray light of the closet, though, she could kind of see it. He had a bit of a scholarly look about him, like you would expect him to know the answers on Jeopardy.

"So why can't you buy food?" Blair inquired.

His broad hand reached up to massage the back of his neck. "When I left my old job, I cashed in my savings to buy myself the time to write. I didn't know how to tell Hazel the truth, so I panicked and told her that I didn't believe in marriage. It was obvious she expected an engagement and I didn't know how to make that commitment when I couldn't be everything she needed me to be. Shortly after that, my rent went up over $1300 a month. Haven't been able to find a roommate." He offered her a small smile. "Turns out your savings don't stretch very far as an artist."

Blair was rooted to the spot, her jaw hanging open like a child. It was like some sort of eerie ghost of Christmas Future warning her what was coming. And the message was delivered from *Mike*, of all people! He had perfectly encapsulated what she knew Hazel's biggest argument would be when she finally found the guts to tell her best friend the truth: Blair was using her savings to backpack through Europe and see as many of the museums as she possibly could. Was it a huge gamble? More than any of the *Mission Impossible* plotlines, but like Tom Cruise's faith in the franchise, Blair felt compelled to make it happen.

The power of speech left her body as Blair gazed up at him like a fish out of water. Was the Universe conspiring for her or against her? She clutched at the black tourmaline bracelet she always wore to protect herself against negative energy. Hazel always called it voodoo, but Blair saw *The Skeleton Key*—she knew what voodoo could do! Right now it comforted her and that was all that really mattered.

"So that's why you said all of that to Hazel?" she finally clarified after several awkward moments. "Because you were afraid she wouldn't support your writing?"

Mike's face contorted as he contemplated his answer. "It wasn't that exactly, although that definitely played a factor. It was more so that I realized my goals no longer aligned with hers and she deserved more. I'll always love Hazel; she's an incredible woman. But I wasn't the right kind of man for the life she's going to get. We would have wound up resentful and unhappy, and I never wanted to feel that way about her."

The logic was sound and Blair discovered a newfound respect for him. It took a lot of guts to stand up to Hazel (Blair knew that better than anybody!), and Mike tried to do it in a way that wouldn't hurt her. She saw him now in a completely different light, instantly regretting her catty thoughts at the beginning of the night.

"But what about you?" Mike suddenly asked. "When are you going to let Hazel down easy and go after what you want?"

Okay, there seriously had to be some kind of voodoo magic at work. How did he know any of that?!

"I...I..." she stammered.

Mike crossed in front of her and squatted down so he could look her in the eyes. "Blair, we both know you were made for more than just pushing out computer graphics."

Brown hair curled slightly around his earnest face. The intensity of his gaze held her own, and despite her embarrassment, Blair recognized the same kind of soul as her own looking out through his gray eyes.

She blushed at being called out. "That's the whole reason we're here tonight," she ultimately admitted.

CHAPTER 7

Mike

He knew that Blair had some kind of secret. She gave the impression of being such an artistic soul, there was no way she was going to survive working day after day on a computer. They really were a lot alike, more so than Mike had initially realized, and it felt like the right time to call her out on her bullshit since Hazel wasn't there to intervene.

Mike had never understood the hold his ex seemed to have over her cousin. Blair was smart, talented, outgoing, and pretty—she had no reason to feel so insecure. Yet whenever the two women got together, it was like Blair shrank into a different version of herself. Maybe Blair needed the push to change things with Hazel just like he did.

The fact that Blair already had a plan in place to do so was a bit of a surprise, but Mike felt oddly proud of her for making that choice. Hazel definitely loved Blair as the pseudo-sister she was, yet that didn't mean they communicated well. The truth had been a long time coming, so if Blair was prepared for that, it was terrific news.

"What are you going to tell her?" he asked.

She swallowed hard and started fidgeting with her fingers before answering him. "I'm leaving for Europe on January First. I already have my ticket for Madrid."

Mike smiled. Going to Europe had always been a dream of his. Hazel didn't like flying over water, so the one trip they had been on was spent doing touristy things in Orlando. Not his idea of travel at all.

He could definitely see someone like Blair fitting in at an outdoor market, wandering around an old city with a sketchbook in hand. He had helped her move into her apartment and hang her paintings on the wall, assuring her at the time they were quite good. Now, he looked back on that moment with a frown. That would have been a better moment to encourage her to pick up a paintbrush again.

Guilt from his decision to make such a drastic career change often led Mike to re-examine his past choices. Life really could change in an instant, as cringy and cliché as that was, and his self-reflection often made him regret not taking different routes when the opportunities presented themselves. His book might already be on shelves and bestseller lists had he gone with his passion earlier in life. Nobody should live with that kind of regret, however, which was usually the thought that swept away the guilt that fostered.

"How long will you be gone?" It must have been a significant amount of time for her to dread telling Hazel. While she might not be willing to fly over water herself, he couldn't imagine his ex-girlfriend making that big of an issue out of Blair going on a European vacation.

Her blush deepened, a shade of red that made her look wanton and made Mike wonder what her face looked like in the throes of an orgasm. He bit hard enough on his tongue to taste blood at the errant thought.

"A year," she explained quietly. "Maybe more." Her eyes were round and full of tears as though she sought his approval for daring such an extreme feat. "I'm going to backpack through as many countries as I can and soak in all of the art I've always wanted to see."

He beamed at her. "That sounds like the best idea I've heard in a long time," Mike assured her. As a consoling gesture, he rubbed her knee. Or, at least, that's what he told himself. It had nothing to do with his sudden desire to feel how silky smooth her skin was.

She visibly relaxed at the words, however, returning his bright smile all the way to the twinkle in her eye and the tension leaving her shoulders. Blair didn't exactly have the most supportive parents, if he remembered correctly. Something about her being biracial made the McAllister family look down on their half-black relative, and her parents placed a lot of pressure on her to succeed as a way to "prove" her worth. Hazel had been the only family member who really gave a shit about her, Mike knew that much. It was probably terrifying to be in her shoes right now, about to head out on an amazing adventure without anyone to lift you up. His respect and admiration for her grew tenfold.

"I wish I had the guts to do what you're about to do," Mike confessed, hoping it would reinforce her belief in herself. "It's so brave."

Her delight was palpable. "Nobody's ever said that to me before."

Mike knew that. Hazel was always too anxious about Blair having a secure future like herself to bother noticing the truth of her cousin's personality. In a city where ambition and financial gain were the driving forces of life, it was beautiful to see somebody break out of that mold. Especially somebody like Blair, who never quite fit into the mold to begin with.

She leaned in closer to him to whisper conspiratorially, "I've been stress eating so much that I can't fit into my pants!" A high pitched squeal of a giggle escaped her glossed lips before she could cover her mouth with her hand.

It was like an invitation to assess her curves, which Mike was not about to turn down. "You're still gorgeous," he breathed. He was afraid of taking things too far and offending her. She would definitely tell Hazel if that happened.

Her eyes softened as she glanced away. "Not like Hazel," she murmured.

"No," he agreed with a scoff. "Gorgeous like only Blair McAllister can be."

Without warning, her gaze darted up to his mouth and he found her lips crashing into his. They were soft and full and a million times better than he had imagined. A vigor like he had never known had him kissing her back, weaving his fingers into her hair to better angle her mouth to his. Her tongue sought refuge in his mouth and must have had Viagra coating it because his dick immediately stood at attention in a way that was almost painful. Kissing with Hazel had never felt like this...

Hazel.

"No, we can't!" He broke apart from her with a roar, taking as many steps back as the small space would allow. His breath was labored like a bull in the ring and he clasped his hands around the back of his head to prevent them from reaching for her.

Blair stood up, allowing the tablecloth across her legs to drop to the floor and reveal her golden thighs. At some point, she had removed her Christmas fishnets and was now bare legged. She shed his cardigan, letting the loose collar of the black t-shirt slide down one shoulder. It left her collarbone exposed and Mike envisioned the reward of tracing kisses along its ascent to her neck. The space was so much warmer, his core body heat rising steadily by the second.

"I'm sorry." Her voice sounded small, as though she was waiting for his reaction. She didn't sound sorry, he noted. "You were just saying all of those nice things, and—"

"True things," Mike interjected firmly. He dropped his hands down to his side and leaned forward to better stare into her eyes. She needed to know how fervently he meant what he said.

"Everything I said was true, Blair."

She paused long enough for the tension to leave her body before launching herself into Mike's arms. This time he shut his mind off and didn't hesitate to wrap one arm around her waist while the other reached down to cup her ass. The lace panties exposed from their movement were taunting him, begging to be ripped from her body so he could fully explore. Her lips were eager, letting his tongue own her mouth this time as she pulled herself closer.

Any space between their bodies felt like a canyon at this point. Before he realized what he was doing, Mike yanked his t-shirt over his head with one hand, loathing that he had to break their kiss to do so. With a groan, Blair copied his movement, removing the ratty concert tee to reveal the perkiest breasts Mike had ever seen. And were those...?

"Your nipples are pierced?" he moaned. All resolve left his body along with it.

Blair grinned mischievously at him. "Among other things."

With a guttural cry, Mike sank down to suckle one nipple in his mouth. His tongue danced with the metal while his hand pinched her other, growing harder by the second at the feel of the warm flesh in his hands. Blair wrapped one leg around his thigh to steady herself and as her passionate cries escalated, she began to grind her hips against his to chase the friction.

Mike's lust grew into a frenzy. The wood he sported demanded to be set free from the confines of his jeans, and although he didn't want to assume sex was on the table, he had to do something to relieve the ache in his groin. However, the moment he pulled his zipper down, Blair fell to her knees and wrapped her tongue around the tip. She spit onto the top of his erection, using it as lube when she wrapped one hand firmly around the base of his shaft while she continued sucking at the head. It was like an out of body experience as she expertly worked him, taking more of him into her mouth as his groans grew louder.

"Please let me fuck that pretty mouth," he growled. He was not above begging, at the moment.

Blair looked up at him through her lashes and smiled wickedly as she nodded around his cock. It was all the permission Mike needed. He laced his fingers through her bouncing blue curls to grip tightly onto her head and thrust his hips forward. When the tip of his dick found the back of her throat, he experienced a spiritual awakening. She lavished her tongue around him, letting the spittle leak out the sides of her mouth. He paused, fearing he had been too rough, but Blair moaned and pushed against his ass with both hands to make him continue.

The act unlocked the next level in him. Pumping furiously, the gurgling sounds from her throat egged him on. A tingling release built at the base of his spine and he ground out, "I'm gonna cum. You better swallow every last drop."

His eyes were blazing as he noticed one of her hands slide into the white lace of her panties to work her clit. The orgasm barreled through him, sending trembles through his body as he emptied into her mouth. Blair guzzled it like a desert nomad desperate for water. She glanced upward, making eye contact with him through her thick lashes, and Mike felt himself instantly grow hard again.

In a single swift move, he twisted himself down to the floor on his back, hauling Blair on top of him. Their kiss tasted salty with his cum and he had to bite down hard on his lip when she leaned back and straddled him, wiping the sides of her mouth with her fingers to lick off what remained.

His eyes dilated with desire and need. Sending her soaring to the same place of nirvana became the only goal in life. "Sit on my face, *NOW*," Mike ordered.

Blair stood up to remove her panties, the lace no longer alluring but an offensive barrier to what he wanted most. From his location on the floor, he could see the glistening arousal dripping from her center. She didn't hesitate, moving to straddle his face, and let out the sexiest sigh he ever heard as he licked the broad side of his tongue along her heat. His tongue lapped against the small metal balls of her clitoral hood piercing, causing them both to cry out in delight.

She began riding his face, leaning back on one hand to roll her hips into the strokes of his tongue. He was so grateful for her dance training because she moved with the fluidity of a woman comfortable with her own body. Wrapping his arms around her thighs to hold her in place, Mike took her clit between his teeth and nipped quick little bites before sucking on the swollen bud.

The sight of her grinding her hips into his face while tugging at her own nipple had all the makings of a porn star's wet dream, and it was enough to make him want to cum again.

With a strangled cry, she came hard against his tongue, shuddering out a few more hip rotations with the climax. They were both panting hard by the time she scooted off his face only to sink herself onto his rock solid cock. It was heavenly to experience Blair's muscles tightening around his shaft. She tugged on his arm, helping him sit upright, before he wrapped an arm around her waist to roll them both so she was on her back with Mike still locked in place between her thighs.

It was Blair who pulled both her legs up over his shoulders, reaching down to play with her clit again. He bent his head down to roll his tongue around the nipple he'd missed sucking on before and with a few quick thrusts and grunts, spent himself inside her. The echoing cries of their dual orgasms faded in the steel room.

Sweat coated both of them as he slowly withdrew, laying down on his back beside her, the length of their bodies pressed together in the tiny space. Common sense flooded his system as he tried to wrap his mind around what they had just done.

I just had the best sex of my life, he thought, *while locked in a closest with Blair McAllister.* Mike closed his eyes against the rush of guilt. Even though he was no longer dating Hazel, she would be devastated if she ever learned what they had done. Panic was setting in, too, because he realized they hadn't used a condom and he had no idea whether or not Blair was on birth control.

Talk about a merry Christmas, he scolded himself.

CHAPTER 8

Alfie

Snow began to fall again, fat, wet snowflakes that clung to Hazel's hair. She looked angelic as they stood on the sidewalk in front of Radio City Music Hall. The streets were still crowded with holiday revelry as it was the time of year that tourists flooded the city to visit all of the Christmas landmarks. New York truly was the city that never slept. Rita had always wanted to experience the magic of a New York City Christmas, but he had watched them bury her body six weeks ago before he had a chance to share it with her.

Alfie knew his parents didn't blame him for her death, but he continued to blame himself. Coming to America was supposed to be the change she needed and when she had finally been brave enough to admit she needed help, fate intervened. The sight of her mangled body in the morgue still haunted his dreams...

No, Alfie reminded himself sternly, *no puedes olvidarte de vivir. You cannot forget to live.* It was the only thing he could

focus on so that his mind didn't succumb to the same dark cloud that followed Rita for most of hers.

"So where exactly are we going?" Hazel asked him, inadvertently redirecting his thoughts to the present moment. There was a beautiful woman at his side. If that wasn't the chance to see some Christmas magic in action, what was?

Alfie grinned at her. "You'll see." He took her by the hand and led her down along the side of the building, which was more of an alleyway than anything.

Trepidation rolled off Hazel in waves. She all but planted roots as they traipsed further away from the crowded street.

Sharply turning, he faced her as he realized, "You never told me your last name?"

Even in the dim lighting of the alley, Hazel's shrewd skepticism cloaked her face. "Will you need it for my Dateline special?"

Alfie just shifted so his weight was on his back leg and gave her an expectant look.

She crossed her arms over her chest in a challenge. "I'm Hazel McAllister. And I'd really appreciate it if you told me where we're going!"

He turned so that he could conceal his triumphant smile. "Come on. This'll be fun, I promise."

Alfie didn't give her a chance to respond before pulling a card out of his pants pocket and swiping it on a lock panel beside the door. The place was so familiar to him that he didn't bother turning on a light, letting habit navigate him forward. Hazel's hand remained clutched firmly in his own, and although she stumbled in the dark a few times, she didn't say a word in protest. Even he could tell this was out of character for her and

Alfie wondered for what felt like the hundredth time that night what was going through her head.

They descended a small set of stairs until arriving at a landing and turning left. Alfie opened another door and flicked on a light.

Hazel's gasp beside him was worth it. He glanced down at her with a small smile as her eyes widened at the sight before them.

Christmas décor surrounded them on all sides. Several fake fir trees lined with powdered snow towered in the back corner, the tops of their peaks bent against the low ceiling. There were snowmen and angels of all sizes, some animatronic, some stationary, stacked precariously on top of one another. A gingerbread house tall enough for them to sit in stood opposite. There were bows, French horns, garland, and lights hanging from the ceiling, and more Santa figurines than Alfie cared to count.

"Where are we?" she asked quietly. He wondered why she spoke so low.

"This is Radio City Music Hall's Christmas storage room," Alfie explained. "These are the decorations not in use at the moment.

Hazel faced him, her eyes frantic with worry. "Alfie, we can't be here! We could get in so much trouble!"

The high pitched nature of her stage whisper made him laugh out loud. "*Aguerrida*, do you think I'd let you get in trouble?"

She glared at him. "This isn't funny, Alfie. I think your idea of trouble is a lot different than mine."

He held up his key card as a reminder. "Would I have this if I wasn't allowed to be here?"

The gears turning in her head were practically visible. "How did you get it?"

Alfie's smile grew. "I work here."

Hazel hadn't expected that answer, he could tell by the way her eyes widened again. She surveyed the room with new interest.

"Come on," he said, taking her by the hand again. Winding back up the stairs and down the hall, they emerged on stage that was set up for the Winter Wonderland theme of that year's Christmas special. The last show had ended only a few hours ago and all of the janitors were about due to leave for the night. There were a few security guards who would prowl the building, but everybody there knew Alfie well enough that they wouldn't bat an eye to him using the space. His boss and the rest of the orchestra had been very understanding about the time off he had taken after his sister's death.

Now, he wove through the set display to reach the upright piano that sat just offstage. Alfie couldn't help but sit down and flex his fingers over the keys, the familiar melody flowing out of him as naturally as his next breath. With his father being one of the most award winning composers in Spain, all musical instruments came easily to him, but piano was by far his favorite. Alfie had dabbled in composition and songwriting in the early stages of his career, finding minor success on his own for two songs he wrote for a couple of his mother's movies, but it wasn't what he wanted long-term. The pressure from his parents to perform and continue the Garza family legacy had been too much, though, so he found himself running away to the United States where hardly anybody knew his familial connections. It had been exciting to finally immerse himself in the music world from the ground up, and he found he enjoyed performing for live shows again when he did so as a nameless part of the general ensemble. Spotlight simply didn't suit him.

Hazel stood beside the piano, one hand resting on the top, her face glowing with joy. She didn't say a word as he morphed the song into a traditional Spanish lullaby. As the final notes punctured the air, Alfie transitioned into a Christmas carol, sticking his tongue out through his cheek to make her laugh.

She giggled, sinking onto the bench beside him, close enough so that their thighs were touching. He let the song die out as they maintained eye contact and the emotions of the moment overwhelmed him. The look in her eyes conveyed awe and magic, like she was just as enraptured as he was. There was a heat between them, a pull of gravity that wanted him to remain in her orbit.

"You're very talented," Hazel finally whispered. Her hand rested on her thigh and Alfie couldn't resist the urge to hold it once more, his tan skin in stark contrast with her pale, creamy color. With a last name like McAllister, she probably had some Irish ancestry, he reasoned.

"If you only knew," he teased her, nudging her shoulder with his.

A laugh escaped before Hazel could hold it in. "Why do you make everything sound so dirty?"

"Baby, I could make it *feel* dirty, too. Don't underestimate me." He winked at her before resuming his position on the piano. Random chords flowed as he composed a song on the spot. It sounded like something happy. Something like the way Hazel made him feel.

His companion merely groaned in response. "See? Right there! Why do you do that?" The exasperation was evident in her tone, alerting Alfie to how thin her patience had become. "Don't you ever want a woman to like you for who you really are?"

Alfie stopped mid-song and faced her. "What makes you think this isn't who I really am?"

She chewed on her bottom lip for a moment before answering. "Because why would someone as kind as you've been to me tonight be such a player? If your only goal was to get in someone's pants, you would have stayed at the party."

This woman was always thinking three steps ahead. "Glad you finally realized what I've been trying to tell you," he teased again.

Standing up, Alfie moved to sit so that his long legs straddled the piano bench and he faced Hazel directly. He smirked as she squirmed underneath his gaze, noting how she clenched her thighs together and her breathing hitched. Whether she wanted to admit it or not, Hazel McAllister was definitely into him.

It was time to use his charisma to his advantage. While he had been truthful when he admitted that he had never had a one night stand, it was not for lack of options. Women had thrown themselves at him since he hit puberty. Thanks to his famous parents, Alfie lived most of his life in the public eye whenever he was home in Spain, and there was never a shortage of women interested in him. That had died down a lot after moving permanently to the United States, but charm was forever engrained in his personality now. He would pull out all the stops if it meant getting Hazel to agree to a real date with him.

"How long have you been playing piano?" Hazel beat him to the punch, her waves cascading down her back and begging him to wrap them around his fist. He imagined she had a secret wild side that came out whenever she had sex. If not, she needed to because the poor woman was as uptight as they came.

He shook his head. "No, we're gonna talk about you," Alfie countered. "I wanna know who my competition is."

Rather than replying, Hazel got up and started walking through the white crystallized trees along the outer perimeter of the stage. Props and other small stage items were arranged just offstage on tables that were neatly numbered so stagehands could quickly orchestrate their appearance and disappearance on stage during shows. Gently, she ran her hand along one of the large bells that hung down from rafters next to the curtains. It was cheap plastic, made to look big and imposing from the back of the auditorium seats, but she looked up at it with pensive reflection as she traced the edge with a finger.

"I actually broke up with someone not that long ago," she finally said, still looking around at all the props and set design. "He was at the party, for some reason. I didn't know he would be there."

Alfie was quiet as he digested this information. The fact that she refused to make eye contact with him made him wonder if the breakup still hurt her. It had been years since he had a serious relationship, and even then, it wasn't that serious. Life changed too fast as a musician to maintain anything committed. He preferred to keep things casual and just let it all unfold.

But that didn't mean he was opposed to something developing further. Hazel seemed like the kind of woman who wanted the white picket fence with 2.5 kids and the scruffy dog. There was nothing wrong with that dream; Alfie himself just hadn't given it any thought. Plans were useless with the lifestyle he led.

"Do you still love him?" Alfie left the bench and approached her slowly where she paused in front of the giant Christmas tree on stage left. She looked even smaller now, with the tree's massive branches ladened with baubles, lights, bows, and tinsel all around her. There were only a few stage lights on for security purposes, but he could have sworn he saw a look of uncertainty flash in her eyes.

"He was a part of my five year plan," Hazel explained with a shrug. "Mike checked off nearly everything on my list."

Alfie narrowed his eyes in confusion. "You have a checklist for love?"

She laughed, though it was a hollow sound. "I have checklists for everything."

"Did you ever think maybe that's the problem?"

Hazel shook her head.

By now, he was directly in front of her, staring down his nose due to their height difference. Alfie smiled gently to let her know he meant no offense when he said, "Love should never have a checklist. It's a verb, not a blue ribbon at the end of a race."

Hazel scoffed. "Yeah, well, not all of us are handsome and talented enough to land any partner we want." She shuffled her feet and diverted her eyes away from the power of his gaze.

Um, what?

She had all of the luscious curves of a Ruben painting and Alfie was clueless as to how she could ever believe a man would reject that. Beauty like hers was something that came around once in a lifetime, with a natural glow, bedroom eyes, and an hourglass shape to die for. If anyone ever told her different, they were either jealous or insane.

"I happen to think you're exquisite," he countered, daring to take a small step closer. There was no space for her to back away while standing so close to the Christmas tree and although a flush crept up her cheeks, she didn't shy away from him. "*Mujer deslumbrante.*"

Dazzling woman.

Hazel merely gulped, looking at him with wide eyes and partially opened lips. They were a ripe red color, flashing like neon signs to beckon him. Although she had stiffened slightly, there was a ray of hope in her eyes indicating she wanted something more.

Ever so slowly, giving her ample time to stop him, Alfie leaned down so that his lips were barely a breath away from hers. "Mistletoe," he murmured, tugging at the branch directly next to her head.

The corners of her mouth turned upward, a soft smile prize as Alfie finally planted his lips on hers as he had been dreaming of doing all night. They were full and firm, and her body melded into his as he drew her closer by the waist.

All of his worries and sadness evaporated as Hazel's warm body anchored him in the joy of the moment. Kissing her was as brilliant as an atomic bomb and he fell headfirst again into her very presence, stunned at the perfection radiating from her soul. Hazel was all things soft and welcoming and good, and Alfie knew in that moment that he couldn't let this be their only night together. He wanted more of these kisses—more of her— and if that meant this night had to last forever, he would make it so.

"Yo, Alf man, is that you?!"

A shining beam of light blared to his right and Hazel jumped away from him as though electrocuted. Her fingers brushed against her bottom lip like she still felt the effects of their kiss the same way Alfie did.

Tony, one of the night security guards, held a bright flashlight towards them like a cop. "What are you doing here, Alfie? You know you aren't supposed to be here, man!"

Hazel whirled on him, hands on her hips again. "I *knew* it!" she cried.

Alfie had a sinking feeling in his stomach and tried to cut Tony off, but didn't open his mouth in time.

"I hope you're doing okay over your sister, dude. We all heard about what happened. So rough…" Tony shook his head sadly and gave Alfie a pitying look.

Hazel's carefully sculpted eyebrows rose in surprise before she glanced at Alfie with concern. The last thing he wanted was her to feel sorry for him, nor had he planned on ever discussing his sister's death with her tonight.

"Yeah, thanks, man," he said to Tony instead, keeping eye contact with Hazel while doing the bro fist bump with the security guard. "We'll just be heading out."

Tony nodded and gave Hazel a small wave. "Have a nice night and again, my condolences, man!" He turned back towards the door leading to the lobby.

Alfie wove his fingers through Hazel's and attempted to steer her offstage to the exit, but she wouldn't budge. Squeezing his hand firmly, her face indicated she was prepared to wait all night for an explanation. She jutted out a hip as if to prove her point.

He let out a resigned sigh. "Let's walk and talk," agreed Alfie.

They walked slowly when they emerged in the alleyway, the snow creating a slush mixture on the ground. She didn't rush him, for which he was grateful, as he tried to find the words to explain what happened to someone who might not understand the significance of his loss.

"My sister Rita was a force of nature," he finally settled on.

They followed 6^(th) Avenue towards Rockefeller Center without any real destination in mind. "She was a model and actress in Spain, considered a great beauty. Not unlike you." Alfie gently nudged her shoulder to try and lighten the moment, but there was a hollowness in the sentiment.

"But with that kind of fame and attention comes a lot of insecurity, scrutiny, and comparison. Our parents were already celebrities, both legendary in their fields, and it was a lot to live up to. The tabloids blew up everything that she did, down to the clothes that she wore and the food that she ordered. If she was spotted having a salad at lunch, everyone speculated she had an eating disorder. If she wore a certain dress, it was because she had a fight with another designer. Rita was under a microscope all the time and it really got under her skin. She—" Alfie's emotions caught in his throat as he tried to swallow thickly. "She wasn't...well. She started having trouble sleeping, stopped laughing and going out with friends, basically just became a shell of herself. My family and I thought maybe some time away would help."

They came up to the ice skating rink set up near the famous Christmas tree in Rockefeller Center and leaned against the wall, facing the skaters. It was easier for Alfie to talk when he couldn't see the pained look in Hazel's eyes as he revealed the tragic truth of what happened to Rita.

"After she came here, though, things got worse. I didn't want to push her, but I could see that she was wasting away. I tried to encourage her to go and get help, I researched facilities that would help her long term, and offered to pay for it so that our parents wouldn't be involved. Rita hated the feeling of disappointing them, like she deserved any blame for being depressed."

Alfie paused because it was the hardest part to admit out

loud, something he still struggled to process. "Rita finally found the will to get help. She texted me and said she was going to go and admit herself at the hospital because she knew she wanted to live and she couldn't get better on her own. On the way there, a car slid on the ice on the road and hit her when she crossed the street, ramming her body into a building when the car finally stopped. The cops tested the driver afterwards and it turned out he was high and hadn't had a driver's license in a long time. I had to go down to the morgue and identify her broken body. They said she didn't suffer."

Tears fell freely down his face as he choked on the last words, caught between laughing and screaming. It destroyed him to know that right when Rita was ready to seek help and address her depression, life had taken her from them anyway. And even though he wasn't responsible for her mental illness or the driver, Alfie felt like he let his parents down by not helping her after he promised things would be different in America. He had only returned from Spain after her funeral a few weeks ago, too miserable to stay and see the effect her death had on his parents.

Suddenly Hazel's head rested on Alfie's shoulder as her arm circled his at the elbow. She didn't say anything, didn't press him to stop crying, or worse—tell him to let it all out, which he despised—but instead simply granted him the patience to work through his feelings in that moment. He appreciated that she wasn't trying to force him one way or another, which was what the grief counselor he had seen tried to do. Losing someone so horrifically after watching them suffer for so long wasn't an easy thing to process; there was never going to be a blueprint for him to follow. Numbness set in over the past few weeks and the spark Hazel ignited was a welcoming relief.

Right now, in that moment, all he wanted was to be present

on a wintry night right before Christmas with a stunning woman like Hazel McAllister. It made him feel *something*, which was so much better than being numb. Standing there in one of the most picturesque, American locations during a time of year that represented love and family, Alfie knew that his hope was what could be called a Christmas miracle.

C'mon, Santa, he thought. *Let me remember what it means to be happy.*

CHAPTER 9

Hazel

Hazel didn't pity Alfie because she could tell that he didn't want anyone's pity. But she recognized the pain in his eye that follows the loss of someone close to you, the loss of a life you intended to share with another person. And while she knew that a breakup was in no way the same as the death of a loved one, she recognized the similar emotion for what it was: grief. He needed her to be there with him in that moment, so that's exactly what Hazel would do.

Twice, she opened her mouth to offer some kind of comforting sentiment, but then closed it after a second thought. It wasn't in her nature to be overly emotional and anything she wanted to say already sounded cliché in her head, so it would have sounded even worse out in the open. Fortunately, death wasn't something she was very familiar with, having never lost someone permanently herself.

Alfie might act like a ladies' man, but Hazel meant what she told him on stage. If going home with a woman was all he had been after, his window for doing so was rapidly closing. It was approaching 1 A.M., and she had no intention of letting anyone seduce her tonight.

Except...that *kiss*.

Hazel had never had the kind of kiss that made your knees go weak and your insides twist like pretzels. His lips had the power to make her question her religion, and despite her stubborn first impression that Alfie Garza was not the kind of man to check off any boxes on The Perfect Partner list, the way her heart continued to pound in his presence made her want to form a new kind of pivot. One where maybe she didn't have to pivot towards a specific goal but a specific feeling.

The thought was as unsettling as it was enticing.

What if Hazel just left herself have tonight? It wasn't like one night of fun and frivolity would banish her entire five year plan. She wouldn't do anything crazy enough to get arrested or any kind of other disastrous consequence, but the prospect of enjoying an entire night with Alfie unencumbered by her lists and goals, without having to worry about whether or not every decision was setting her on the right path for her perfect future, or even stopping to consider how many aspects of Alfie's personality fit into her Perfect Partner. Right now, Hazel didn't need him to be her perfect partner; she didn't even *want* him to be. She simply wanted to spend a night laughing and feeling good, and somehow with all his innuendos and smirks, Alfie Garza made her experience both.

Her stomach picked that moment to give an embarrassing gurgle. She tried to wrap an arm around herself to shield the noise, but Alfie definitely heard. He stood up straighter and looked down at her with a knowing smile.

"When's the last time you had something to eat today?" he asked.

She shrugged. "I skipped dinner because I knew we were going to the party, but then I never ate anything at the party since I was only there a whopping total of 30 minutes."

He pretended to look wounded, clutching one hand to his heart and contorting his lips playfully. "I can't have you starving yourself, *aguerrida*. Let's go get something to eat."

A blush bloomed across Hazel's cheeks. She hated eating in front of people. When you're plus sized, everyone judged you for what you ate, whether it was healthy or not. "I'm not starving myself. I'll be fine."

Alfie leaned down so that he was looking her dead in the eye. Clasping both of her hands in his, he said, "Baby, I can't have you losing a single curve on this gorgeous body because someday I'm going to lick every inch of you with my tongue. Now where are we going to eat?"

No one had ever spoken to her like that before. Hazel felt her entire body burning as the image of a sex god like Alfie licking and exploring her body. It made her mouth water in an entirely different kind of hunger.

She remembered what she promised herself about letting go just for tonight and decided to admit the truth. "I'd really like something sweet."

He grinned at her. "I know just the place!"

After another brief argument on the merits of an Uber versus the subway, Hazel emerged from the black sedan in front of a tiny shop front with glowing neon lights declaring it The Donut Pub. A floor to ceiling window displayed puffy donuts, croissants, and muffins.

"You're gonna love this place, *aguerrida*," Alfie insisted, holding open the door for her and waving her in.

It smelled like cinnamon sugar inside. There were bows and

garland strung around all of the displays and a giant wreath hung on a door that led to the back. A statuesque black woman greeted them from behind the counter with a smile.

"Be there in a minute, Cassia," Alfie chirped with a nod. "We've got ourselves a Donut Pub virgin over here."

Hazel didn't even bother to react because she was too busy salivating over the colorful rows of donuts. There were standard flavors, but also fun flavors like birthday cake, Fruity Pebbles, and s'mores. An entire case had letter donuts in bright holiday colors with sprinkles.

"Ooh, let's spell out one of our names!" she squealed in delight. She tried to ignore the giant smile Alfie bestowed upon her and continued examining the various flavors.

"Should we use my full name so we have more letters?" he offered with a grin.

Hazel shoved him playfully but inquired, "What's your full name?"

"In Spain, my full name is Juan Alfredo Joaquin Herman de Garza," he explained. "We use a lot of family names there. Here, all my paperwork just says Alfredo Garza. Alfie is easier."

With a grin, Hazel turned to the woman behind the counter and said proudly, "Please spell out ALFREDO in donuts!"

"Oh no!" taunted Alfie, pushing to stand in front of her and block her path to the employee. "I want HAZEL in donuts with custard filling!"

Cassia just laughed at them both and said, "Coming right up!"

Alfie tugged on Hazel's coat to pull her close and whispered in her ear, "I can't wait to eat you."

Hazel's face blushed to her hairline, but she leaned back enough to look him in the eye and mumble, "I hope I taste good."

She was rewarded when his eyes darkened and he bit down on his bottom lip. His warm brown eyes perused the length of her body again, only this time Hazel didn't mind so much. She kind of liked the idea that he was pleased with what he saw.

Their donuts were boxed and handed over after Hazel lost the battle of payment at the register. Alfie winked at the employee behind the counter as he insisted, "It's my job to treat the queen."

He steered them towards the barstools looking out onto a New York night that sold tourists on winter attractions. It was beautiful to see the smiling faces walking through heavy snowflakes, not yet piled high enough to make people stay indoors. They were in the West Village part of the city, a borough known for its artistic, bohemian residents. It was the part of the city Blair always wanted to frequent, although it made sense for a musician like Alfie to seem so at home in the neighborhood.

Hazel felt a pang of guilt that she hadn't checked her phone for messages from her cousin. As she pulled her cell out of her pocket, however, she frowned when the screen lit up. Not a single missed call or waiting text. That wasn't like Blair at all. She was just about to say so to Alfie and suggest they return to his place and check on her, when he broke up her thoughts with a moan that sent tingles straight to her pussy.

"You taste incredible!" Alfie stage whispered in a groan, the custard filling sticking to the facial hair around his lips.

She laughed playfully and threw a napkin at his face.

He wiped off the remnants with a smirk and said, "At least the front of you does. I'll get to the back half in a minute!" The roguish wink that followed promised he meant what he said.

It was a scandalous thought. "You wouldn't really...would

you?" Hazel was half appalled, half aroused picturing Alfie bending her over his lush bed and putting his head *there*.

"Oh, *aguerrida*," Alfie murmured, leaning in close and locking eyes with her as his fingers brushed along her jawline, "there's nothing about your body I don't want to explore."

She was pretty certain she flushed all the way to her toes. Sex was never something her family talked about, and although her parents were still happily married, they had never been the type of couple to display affection openly. It wasn't until college that Hazel learned other couples were more public with their physical intimacy. None of that mattered after she met Mike because his speed matched hers. Their sex life had been perfectly satisfactory.

But Alfie's teasing made her wonder if sex could be more than that. If Alfie's lips touching other parts of her body would make her feel as alive and beautiful as they did when he kissed her on stage. What if it was a one time fluke? What if she never felt that kind of passion and recklessness ever again?

As she looked up at him and he gave her another sexy smirk before biting into the Z of her name, however, she sincerely doubted it. Everything the man did sent a wave of arousal straight between her thighs. And Hazel desperately wanted to relieve that feeling.

Throwing caution to the wind almost didn't sound so scary with Alfie. He had really opened up to her, a vulnerability that she found not only refreshing but real. New York was filled with phony people who wanted fame or fortune (usually both) and it was kind of draining to deal with some of their personalities, especially with her job in marketing. Multi-million dollar clients were often exhausting and unreasonable in their demands and over the top personas. It sounded like Alfie came from that world and actively rejected it.

Hazel wasn't familiar enough with foreign cinema to recognize his name, but there must have been a lot of fame surrounding his parents if his sister felt that kind of pressure to perform for the public eye all the time. Yet Alfie was completely relaxed and at home sitting in a 24 hour donut shop in the middle of the night. He blended in with the rest of the patrons and must have been a regular given how familiar he was with the clerk behind the counter. Alfie was simply himself, without any pretense, and it was the most attractive trait she had discovered.

Before she had time to question herself or allow common sense to take over her mouth, she lowered her voice seductively to comment, "Pretty sure I will taste better than that donut," and smiled coyly at him.

She was rewarded with a growl, the multi-colored brown hue of his eyes darkening with lust. "*No hagas promesas que no puedas cumplir, aguerrida,*" Alfie murmured. *Don't make promises you can't keep.*

"*Tendrás que descubrir mi farol,*" Hazel replied. *You'll have to call my bluff.*

Alfie smashed the top of his donut box down and pinned it to his chest, using his free hand to grab hers and pull her out of the chair.

"Wait-what about my donuts?!" she cried in a laugh.

"I'll bake you all the donuts you want when we're done!" he replied, his voice thick with lust. He already had his phone out with the Uber app pulled up, ordering a car. "Your place or mine?"

Embarrassment flooded her cheeks, though he thankfully

didn't ask the source. As bold as Hazel felt from throwing caution to the wind, shame would not let her take him back to Blair's apartment and the tiny twin bed she had been forced to sleep on since she broke up with Mike. "Yours is fine," she whispered.

If he noticed the way her voice caught in her throat, Alfie didn't let on, but he wrapped an arm around her to pull her close. Snowflakes were falling and catching on her eyelashes as she craned her head upwards to look at him. His eyes twinkled a way that promised both mischief and sex, and they were fixed on her. One hand brushed the hair back from her face before he leaned down to kiss her again.

This kiss packed just as much of a punch as the first, making Hazel's body tingle all the way down to her toes. She vaguely recalled the scene from the 80's romcom *Pretty in Pink* that Blair made her watch where Molly Ringwald's character discussed strong lips and knew Alfredo Garza's lips would qualify. He owned the moment, keeping her body tightly against his, while gently caressing his thumb on her cheek. It succeeded in soothing her nerves and rekindled the passion she felt before.

One night—she would allow herself one night.

CHAPTER 10

Blair

What. Just. Happened.

Blair struggled to control her breathing now that the throes of passion were over and the consequences of her actions were brandishing her in the face. She just had sex with Mike Downey, of all people! Hazel would have a conniption if she found out!

It wasn't intentional for her to throw herself at him like that. Mike was being so sweet and understanding, supportive in a way that Blair desperately wanted someone in her life to be, and she got swept up in the heat of the moment. Turns out someone only needed to mutter a few pretty words and she would spread her legs like she was in dance practice.

The fact that both orgasms rocked her world didn't really make it any better, although it definitely made her eager to go back for more. Mike was the last person in the world she would have expected that kind of tongue work from, but maybe men really did have the closet kinks like Cosmopolitan would lead her to believe. He certainly made her body feel better than any other partner she had ever had.

But how in the world could she keep something like this from Hazel? Blair was already on the verge of an eating disorder from the stress of hiding her European trip from her cousin; this might very well give her a heart attack at the ripe young age of 24! She needed to figure something out before she destroyed their relationship completely.

She shifted half an inch away from Mike to prevent their skin-to-skin contact and hastily pulled a tablecloth over her body as she sat up. After a moment, Mike sat upright, too, drawing up his knees to lean his elbows on while both of them stared straight ahead. Neither said anything and the silence was deafening with the weight of their collective guilt.

"We have to tell Hazel," he finally said, breaking the tension with a tremor in his voice.

Blair let out a hollow laugh. "You're higher than giraffe nuts if you think for one second I'm going to tell Hazel. Not a chance." She tried not to let the fact that his first thoughts had been of her cousin sting, but she couldn't help feeling affronted.

Mike leaned forward and hastily grabbed his pants, yanking them on as he stood up. He faced her in a panic as he struggled with his zipper. "How can we not? What if you're pregnant?! I've never been this reckless in all my life!"

His point shattered another bubble in Blair's mind. They hadn't used any protection and she wasn't on birth control. It had always seemed like a waste when she didn't have a boyfriend and didn't want to deal with potential side effects. Now the warning label was mild in comparison to the image of a wailing infant lying in her arms that dominated her thoughts. A baby would cancel any possibility of her European tour.

She shook her head to clear her thoughts, standing up while holding the tablecloth in front of her body. A box to her right contained more clothes and although the sweatpants she withdrew had stains on them, they barely registered with her brain as she pulled them on before snatching the black t-shirt from the ground. "We won't get pregnant," she whispered, more to assure herself than anything else, as she dragged the tee over her head.

"Are you on birth control?" Mike asked hopefully.

Blair's cheeks reddened. "No," she begrudgingly admitted, "but I won't let myself have a baby right now. I can't even take care of myself."

Mike sighed before tugging on his own shirt. "No offense, but that's not exactly comforting."

"Oh, I'm sorry!" she burst out. "I forgot that I need to be comforting *you* in this situation! Not only did I break my best friend's heart, but I might have permanent proof of the act all because a good looking guy spouted some nice words to me!" Blair huffed in her frustration.

He had the decency to look repentant. "Blair, that's not what I meant. I'm not placing any blame because this was just as much my fault, but we kinda need to talk about this." Mike held up his hands in surrender.

She was moving towards hysterics. "We don't need to talk about anything, Mike!" Blair burst out angrily. "I just need to freak out for a minute so I can panic and then figure out what to do."

Mike's face cringed. "So now women panic after having sex with me. You really know how to build up a man's ego."

Audacity was at an all time high inside their steel box, and Blair gripped her black tourmaline bracelet tightly as she counted to ten in her head. Yelling at him might make her feel better in the short term, but they had enough problems barreling their way without starting a war between them.

"You're right, Mike," Blair finally settled on, her voice sickly sweet. "My sole job right now is to make sure you feel like the sex gift to women you envision yourself to be. Betraying my only real family and not using birth control is small potatoes in comparison to your lowered self-esteem."

She could tell when the light bulb clicked on because Mike's entire demeanor changed. Embarrassment flooded his face and his shoulders slumped. "I'm sorry for being such a jackass. I'm not thinking straight at the moment."

It was laughable to assume that she was even thinking at all right now. How had she let something like this happen?! Blair couldn't decide which was worse, the hurt she had willingly inflicted on her best friend and cousin or the possibility of an unplanned pregnancy with said best friend's ex that would force her to cancel the dream trip of a lifetime? If there was an award for the Worst Human in Existence, Blair would have won by a landslide.

She sank back down and cradled her knees to her chest, rocking slightly on her heels, as she considered all of her options. Telling Hazel had to be her number one priority, right after they figured out a way to leave this godforsaken closet. Worrying about a pregnancy would take a backseat because there was just as much of a possibility that they didn't get pregnant. And if nothing else, it would serve as a warning to get a giant box of condoms for her suitcase before Blair left for Spain. If Mike Downey could whisper a few niceties and get her out of her pants, she would be a goner for a shirtless foreigner speaking in a Romance language.

"Look," Mike began, gently sliding down to sit beside her, "we'll figure it all out together. We both did this, and we both care about Hazel. It's only fair that we both tell her the truth."

He reached out as though he was about to take her hand and then thought better of it.

Blair shook her head. "Hazel will never forgive me." Tears filled her eyes at the prospect. Hazel was the only person in her family who ever made her feel like she belonged, even compared to her own parents. Their friendship went deeper than deep; it was a bonded sisterhood forged with magic stronger than a pair of mystical jeans.

Sympathy washed over Mike's features. It didn't resemble pity, but it gave Blair a sour taste in her mouth all the same.

"Hazel loves you. Believe me, I spent a good majority of our relationship listening to her anxiously worrying over you. If anything, she'll never forgive me," Mike countered. "I'll forever be the asshole who broke her heart and then seduced her cousin."

Blair's laughter rang out in the confined space despite her sadness over the situation. "That was *quite* the seduction."

Grinning, he nodded. "Yep, that's me. Just a regular Rico Suave charming ladies out of their panties." Playfully, Mike nudged his shoulder into hers.

She laughed again. "I never would've believed it if I hadn't seen it with my own eyes," vowed Blair. "You may keep my panties as a souvenir." Leaning forward, she plucked the ruined lace off the floor and wadded them into Mike's palm.

His eyes darkened momentarily with lust before looking away. "More like a trophy," he commented lightly, though his voice sounded tight.

Her heart swelled. "Don't say things like that."

Mike's eyebrows lifted in surprise. "Why not?"

"Because it's going to be hard enough to forget how good you made me feel," Blair admitted.

As if drawn to her by a magnet, Mike leaned closer, the ghost of his breath caressing her lips. "You want to forget?" he murmured.

Longing filled his deep gray eyes and she shuddered as she drew closer, just as drawn to him as he was to her. There was too much static in the air, a current pulling them together despite the lack of air flow in the metal box they occupied, but Blair didn't want to stop it. Guilt tried to push its way through but she refused to let herself feel anything other than the gravity pulling her towards him.

It was so wrong on so many levels. Two wrongs wouldn't make a right...

"But three rights make a left," Blair argued in a breathless whisper, her lips nearly brushing Mike's.

"What?" he asked.

She didn't have a chance to respond. Instead, their lips connected in a kiss once more and everything else faded into the background.

Being stuck in her co-worker's closet would either be the best or worst thing that ever happened to her. Maybe Santa was sending her a Christmas miracle, after all.

CHAPTER 11

Mike

In some part of his brain, Mike knew that making out with Blair McAllister again, especially after their lame attempt at justifying the chaos they had just created, was not the smartest decision. Making seemingly dumb decisions was now part of his daily routine, however, so he found himself past the point of caring. Besides, why would anything else matter when her lips were strong enough to root him to the spot…

No.

"We really shouldn't be doing this!" Mike pulled away, covering his mouth with his hand as though that would prevent things from heating up again. He had to physically turn his body to face away from her to get the words out. Seeing her shoulders sink with disappointment made his resolve crumble, but he also knew he wasn't this kind of guy. He would never intentionally hurt someone he cared about, and even if he and Hazel were no longer a couple, something like this would destroy her. Not to mention, Mike was far past the day and age where one night stands and meaningless hookups held any appeal.

"I know. I'm sorry!" Blair's voice had a pleading note to it that made Mike turn around to check on her. She was visibly shrinking into the version of herself that always existed around her cousin, and Mike hated it.

He sighed. "You have nothing to be sorry for," began Mike, "but I'm not that guy, Blair. I'm not the guy to sleep around and make someone feel bad about themselves because of it. The last thing I want to do is make Hazel feel any more insecure than she already does, and I'd rather stay locked here in this closet forever than to ever make you feel less than the gorgeous woman you are. Can you honestly tell me that won't happen after this?"

Blair laughed, the kind of hysterical sounds indicating disbelief. Or insanity. Mike wasn't entirely sure.

"I have absolutely zero expectations of what's going to happen after this!" she finally burst out after her laughter died down. "I'm leaving for a year long trip in less than ten days, Mike!"

He frowned at that. The moment got too hot and heavy before he had a chance to consider the fact that she was leaving the country. While that part made it easier to hide their rendezvous from Hazel, it also left a small part of him saddened; he didn't want whatever this was to end so soon.

"So this is it?" Mike asked for the sake of clarity. "We only have tonight?"

Blair nodded solemnly. "It's not like we could ever have a relationship, Mike. You're my best friend's ex."

She took another step backward, wrapping her arms around her body for warmth. It wasn't enough space between them to quell the anxiety starting to form in Mike's chest. Her words made sense in a rational way—obviously they couldn't be in a relationship given their history. But that didn't stop the desperation he felt to be inside her once again. A yearning that grew exponentially by the second as he stared at her in the tiny space.

Mike's intent wavered for a fraction of a second before he crossed in front of her in a single stride. "Then I guess we better make tonight count," he growled before planting his lips on hers once more.

Blair didn't hesitate as she jumped on him. He grabbed her ass, pulling her muscular thighs around his torso, and shoved her back against the shelves. Several of the items clattered as the shelf slammed into the wall, but Blair only moaned her approval. He suspected she liked it rough, granting him the opportunity to tap into his wildest fantasies. It was an aspect of his sexuality he always wanted to explore and never could without the appropriate partner. If one night with Blair was all he was going to get, he wanted to make it a night they would never forget.

Leaning back, he yanked the t-shirt over her head again, using one hand to massage her breast and pinch her upright nipple. Mike loved how the flesh filled his hand, warm and soft, enticing him to lick every inch of her skin. His erection was thickening in his pants again, straining against the zipper, urging him to return to her wet heat once more.

As if echoing his thoughts, Blair broke away from their kiss long enough to pant, "You aren't getting near this kitty unless your tool is wrapped!"

Mike groaned in frustration. The hand that had been kneading her tit wrapped back under her ass to provide more support as he lowered them both back down to the ground. He tugged at her pants, but she swatted his hands away so she could yank down his. They were bunched together at his knees where he hovered over her. Blair was on her back underneath him, her blue-streaked curls creating a halo around her head.

As soon as his cock sprang free, she slid her hand through her pussy, using her own arousal as a lubricant when she wrapped her hand firmly around his shaft. The sight was so erotic, Mike practically came then and there. Blair grinned up at him with the tip of her tongue poking out as though she could tell.

Lust consumed Mike's every thought. She looked so damn sexy underneath him, sweat covering her in a glittery sheen from the weak light in the closet. He pulled back to lower himself down to her pussy. Arousal already leaked down her thigh, and he could smell the cum from their previous tryst. She was completely bare, whether from waxing or shaving, he couldn't tell, but he loved the sight of her tan skin unencumbered by pubic hair. Everything about her was exquisite, the most glorious gift from Santa he had ever received.

Oh, yes. Tonight would be the best Christmas present of his life. Mike wrapped his tongue around her clit in joy.

CHAPTER 12

Alfie

Hazel's knee jittered against Alfie's on their Uber ride back to his place. He kept her hand locked firmly in his own, using his thumb to rub comforting circles on top. They kept their gazes locked on one another, and if it weren't for the obvious longing in her eyes, Alfie would interpret her anxious tick as a sign of refusal. It wasn't that she was anxious at the thought of being forced or acting against her own desires, however, it was that she was eager to end the anticipation.

Alfie had no idea how much he tipped their driver as he flung a wad of cash into the front passenger seat, but the moment his front door came into view, all bets were off and Alfie's mouth crashed into Hazel's. Every kiss with her felt more monumental than the last, and it was a heady spiral Alfie never wanted to stop. Hazel McAllister intoxicated him, and as startling as it was to feel so much after not feeling anything for so long, it didn't terrify him like he thought it would.

Neither of them was willing to break the kiss long enough to properly remove clothing, so their jackets were flung across the back of an armchair. Hazel tried to steer Alfie towards the couch, but he shook his head against her mouth.

"You're not some easy piece of ass and this isn't about me scoring," he murmured between passionate kisses, her pants of desire lighting a fire within him. "If we're doing this, you're going to be in my bed, where you belong, and you don't leave until the sun rises, *aguerrida.*"

Hazel whimpered her assent as her knees threatened to buckle against him. Her eyes were round as quarters, illuminated with lust and excitement. She bit down on her bottom lip before nodding. If she had any misgivings, Alfie couldn't tell, and the prospect of her submission only made the night that much more enticing to him. Scooping one arm under her knees and another behind her back, Alfie started to carry her upstairs like they were newlyweds on their wedding night.

She immediately began bucking in protest. "Alfie, I weigh too much! Put me down!"

He stopped abruptly in the middle of the stairs, glaring down his nose at her. "Baby, listen to me when I say, you will not leave that bedroom until I have ingrained in that beautiful head of yours that you are a goddess."

A flush crept over her features, turning her face flaming red. The sentiment made her squirm in his arms, but his resolve didn't falter. It was unfathomable to Alfie that a woman as stunning as Hazel hadn't learned everything she had to offer. He couldn't help but wonder if the ex that sent her into a tailspin earlier in the night was the root of the problem.

Before he could ask, however, she argued, "That sounds like a tall order for one night."

Alfie grinned at her. "Who says it's gonna be just one night, baby?"

They reached the landing a moment later and Alfie kicked open the door to his bedroom before gently laying her down on the bed. He climbed next to her, allowing his body to press against the entire length of hers, and kissed her softly. She smelled amazing and looked like an angel across his comforter. A Christmas angel, no doubt sent from Rita, to brighten his spirits over the holiday season when he needed it most.

"I say it can only be one night," Hazel whispered sheepishly. Pink still lingered in her cheeks, but she maintained eye contact with him when she said it to prove her earnestness. "I have a five year plan, Alfie, and I won't give that up."

It only served to make Alfie that much more enamored with her. Hazel was so different from the other women he had dated, and although he barely had the next five days planned, he found himself wanting to see if there was room in her five year plan for someone like him. A question like that would probably make Hazel run from him in a panic, but Alfie bit down on the inside of his cheek to stop himself from asking. One night could never be enough to explore all of the possibilities that existed between them.

There was only one thing he could do. Make her utterly and completely infatuated with him before the end of the night so that she saved his number in her phone and agreed to a second date.

With that goal in mind, Alfie deepened the next kiss, using his tongue to explore her mouth. He moved to hover over her, one hand creeping underneath his hoodie she wore to find her breasts. A low growl escaped when he discovered she didn't have on a bra.

Hazel, for her part, mewled in delight at his ministrations. She gripped his biceps so firmly that her nails created crescent moons in his skin, and Alfie reveled in the pain. The only light in the room came from the holiday decorations outside streaming through the windows, which wasn't enough for him. He wanted to see her in all her luscious glory as he made her come as many times as possible.

Flicking on the bedside table lamp, Alfie retreated off the bed to unbutton his dress shirt. Hazel's eyes darkened with lust as she propped herself up on her elbows to watch. Her teeth sank into her bottom lip as he moved to the last button, inflating his ego, and he shrugged out of the shirt slowly. He gave her a second to take in his broad shoulders and muscular arms before peeling the tank top undershirt off. A shuddering gasp escaped her as Alfie moved to undo his belt, and he couldn't help but flex a little bit to try and show off his ab muscles. The gym had become a second home to him on the nights when he couldn't sleep since Rita's death, which meant he spent a few hours there nearly every night, and it was clearly paying off based on Hazel's response. Alfie vowed to spend a thousand hours there over the course of the next year if it led to more of the heated gazes on her face right then.

Wanting to build on the moment, Alfie was agonizingly slow to pull off his tailored dress pants and boxer briefs. His dick was so hard it was painful, his balls heavy with the need for release. There was an audible gulp from Hazel when his cock finally sprang free and he couldn't help but smirk at her. For once, words failed him because seeing the look of awe and excitement she was sending him negated any charming or arrogant joke that occurred to him. There was only this moment, just the two of them, and the rest of the city faded to black.

Alfie stepped forward and gently pulled at the waistline of Hazel's leggings, parting her legs enough that he could stand between her knees at the edge of the bed. Neither of them broke eye contact as he carefully drew the leggings down, allowing his fingertips to brush along the bottom of her thighs in the process, before letting them pool on the floor. She surprised him by leaning forward to kiss him lightly on the lips and then crossed her arms over her chest to grip the hem of his hoodie and pull it over her head.

Hazel's voluptuous breasts were even better than Alfie imagined. Landing face first in them at his neighbor's party wasn't enough to do them an ounce of justice. Hourglass curves taunted him and he unintentionally let a loose chuckle escape as he drank in the sight of her.

She grinned. "Is there something funny?"

Alfie smiled back. "Just wondering how Santa knew exactly what I wanted for Christmas this year."

Hazel's grin widened and she leaned forward to wrap her arms around his neck. Alfie climbed back onto the bed, kissing her deeply as he reveled in the feeling of her beneath him. It was sheer bliss, the very best kind of dream, and he never wanted to wake up. There was only the thin strap of her red thong between them, already soaked with her need for him, and with one sharp tug, the fabric broke.

"You won't be needing this anymore," he whispered playfully as Hazel's eyes widened in shock. She laughed outright, the same joyous sound that made Alfie's heart sing earlier in the night. He reached down to swipe one finger through her pussy before groaning into her neck. "Baby, you are dripping for me!"

"I'm sorry! This is all just so sexy!" Hazel's face crumpled in confusion and embarrassment, making Alfie want to kick himself for his commentary.

"It's a good thing!" he comforted her. "You're the sexiest,

most beautiful woman I've ever seen, and I can't believe I'm lucky enough to catch your eye. I won't waste a single moment of tonight, *aguerrida*, so erase all of your doubts and insecurities. You are what every woman should aspire to be and I won't let you leave this bedroom until there isn't a thought in your head that will tell you otherwise."

His lips began to work their way down to her breasts as he poised his thumb against her clit. Thankfully with his weight still on top of her, Hazel's bucking wasn't a deterrent. She whimpered as his tongue found her nipple, erect and perfect, while he thrust a sole finger into her cunt. It was so tight that Alfie momentarily wondered if she had lied to him about her virginity, but once his thumb began circling her clit again, Hazel's muscles relaxed enough that it no longer felt like a death grip.

He paused to look up at her, keeping his mouth right at her nipple. "*Aguerrida*, you have to trust me if you want to enjoy this." Hazel flushed at his plea. "Let go of every thought in your head. Live in this moment, as I am."

She nodded in understanding and thrust her hips upward to indicate that she wanted him to continue his play. Her eyes closed with a low moan as Alfie added a second finger, keeping his thrusts slow and shallow.

Hazel's mind was at war with her lust and he didn't want her to end up regretting their night. Inspiration and desire flooded him with an idea. Alfie darted off the bed and into his closet to snatch a tie off the shelf inside before returning to a wide-eyed Hazel. He navigated her to the center of the bed, drawing her hands over her head to use the tie around her wrists.

"Wha-what are you doing?" Hazel sputtered as he tightened the knot against his headboard.

"I'll untie you when you let go," Alfie replied with a smile.

She returned the smile, although with a hint of trepidation still mixed in. Alfie popped a fierce kiss on her mouth before grabbing her hips and flipping her over. Hazel yelped in alarm, which only made his grin widen. He pulled up on her hips and positioned her on her knees so that her entire backside was exposed to him.

Her ass was every bit as wide and luscious as he predicted, and he bit down on his tongue to stifle a moan. The resulting pause made Hazel squirm.

"Please don't look at my butt!" she cried. "I have cellulite!"

Alfie spanked her right cheek sharply. "I think you mean 'seasoning' because this is about to taste like heaven!"

The shock of his words made Hazel yank on her wrist restraints and try to catch his eye over her shoulder. "You wouldn't dare! I thought that was a joke!"

"Baby, I will never joke about sex with you!" he countered.

Her brown waves were flinging everywhere from how hard she shook her head. "I don't think I'm ready for that! You shouldn't look at me from this angle!"

More so to calm her down than anything, he returned his fingers to her wet cunt and started his slow thrusts again, using his other hand to massage her left ass cheek. Alfie tried to keep his voice firm but soothing as he promised her, "I *want* to see you from every angle, Hazel. I can't even say something stupid like 'cellulite doesn't bother me' like other men probably said because that implies there is something to be bothered by. I swear to you, on the heart of my sister, every part of you is sexy and turning me on right now. Can I please rock your world and prove it to you?"

A tearful-sounding laugh escaped her lips as the tension left her shoulders. "Do you mean that? Truly?"

Alfie nodded. "Every word."

"Nobody's ever talked to me like this before," Hazel admitted quietly after a moment.

A shot of emotion stronger than Alfie could name went straight to his heart. "Then you better get used to it," he replied, "because I'm gonna remind you everyday from here on out." With that, Alfie added a third finger and thrust further into her pussy, accelerating his pace as he planted another hard spank across her ass. She cried out in delight and he bent his head down to place wet, languid kisses on her tailbone, dragging his tongue down across his handprint. He felt her stiffen as he drew closer to her ass crack. Without lifting his head, Alfie murmured a reminder against her soft skin, "Every angle, *aguerrida*."

Using his free hand to gently part her cheeks, he increased the pace in her pussy and pushed his thumb down harder on her clit and blew lightly on her asshole. The moans that escaped her needed to be recorded because that was now the only sound he ever wanted to wake up to. Alfie smiled at the thought.

Flattening his tongue, he started at the bottom of her tailbone and trailed downward. Even now, after everything they had done in the course of the night, Hazel's skin smelled like brown sugar cinnamon, and she tasted divine. His tongue circled around the hole before tenderly massaging his thumb at the entrance, pooling his saliva on his finger. Her body relaxed, leaving her back door unclenched, and he promptly slid the tip of his thumb inside. There was no point in even asking if she had ever done anal sex before, but she surprised both of them with her panted cry, "God, YES!" as he plunged deeper inside.

There was no reason to hide his triumphant smile since she couldn't see it anyway. Instead, Alfie withdrew both hands long enough to reach into the bedside table drawer and take out a condom. Sheathing himself, he lined the tip of his cock at her entrance and used both hands to part her ass cheeks again, baring the puckered hole to him like a prize. She mewled in delight and thrust her hips backward.

"Please, Alfie!" Hazel whimpered.

"I'm gonna try something, baby," he said. "Do you trust me?"

"Whatever you want!" she cried out, pulling again at the restraints on her wrists.

No further encouragement was needed. Alfie thrust his dick into her in one smooth motion at the same time he sheathed his index finger in her ass. Pushing down with his finger gave him a delicious sensation against his cock, which was already in a vice grip from Hazel's pussy. Ecstasy had him in a chokehold because this was pure bliss, a level of nirvana unlocked that Alfie never wanted to leave.

The tempo of his thrusts increased as Hazel's moans crescendoed. Her knuckles were white as she held onto the tied knot on his headboard, her light brown waves cascading over one shoulder as she ground her ass further into him. His dick was as hard as steel and he could feel the tingling sensation building in his balls, signaling he was ready to come. Alfie firmly grabbed onto her hips, inwardly salivating over how well they fit in his hands, and pushed her thighs closer to tighten down on him.

A loud queef erupted through the room on the next thrust, blaring like a trumpet between them.

CHAPTER 13

Hazel

A queef?!

A frickin' queef?!

How was Hazel supposed to come back from this? She had been in the middle of the most mind-blowing sex of her entire life, preparing for the orgasm on the brink of barreling through her, and that one little moment of preparation downstairs led to a goddamn vagina fart on the sexiest man alive's throbbing cock!

There was no way to pivot from a situation like this. She was literally tied to his bed, unable to move or remedy the horrific aftermath, and she didn't know what to do. Her back had arched up like a cat, her body frozen in disgusted shock, and Alfie had paused with his cock still buried inside her. It was worse than her worst nightmare!

A tense silence followed her body's traitorous sound, then Alfie began to laugh. Not a small, simple chuckle either. It was a hearty belly-laugh; a deep guffaw that made his entire body shake as he doubled over her back, wrapping both his arms around her hips and holding her tight. He laughed so hard that

Hazel felt the tears slide down his nose and onto her exposed skin.

Desperately, Hazel prayed for a meteor to crash into the room. Aliens to descend. Dorothy's house to make a grand re-entrance. Literally anything to take the focus off her body's gross betrayal and stop the humiliation developing rapidly by the second as he continued to laugh around her. She could not think of a single moment that had ever embarrassed her more, including the time she walked around the mall at 15 years old with her skirt tucked into her underwear.

Frantically she began tugging at the tie binding her to the headboard, trying to escape its hold so she could bolt out the door. The more she struggled, the more the knot tightened, and she let out a tearful whimper at her predicament.

The movement caught Alfie's attention, however, and he leaned up while stifling his laugh to hold one of her hands. "What are you doing?" he exclaimed as Hazel's yanking started to rock the bed.

"Please let me go, Alfie!" begged Hazel. "I am absolutely mortified and-"

"Mortified?" he echoed "Why, baby? Your body is cheering us on, and that's sexy as hell!"

Despite her embarrassment, Hazel let out a weak, watery laugh at his assessment. Alfie joined her, massaging her lower back as their laughter grew until neither of them could contain themselves. She collapsed on the bed, the pillow muffling her joy, with Alfie landing beside her in his own fit of glee. It was an odd angle since her arms were still pinned above her head, but they were both too far gone to care.

Alfie wrapped a leg over her thighs, spooning her back, and kissed the top of her head through his chuckles. After a few minutes he noticed her predicament with the headboard and pulled at the end of the tie to loosen it. Hazel massaged her wrists as soon as her hands sprang free, rolling over to face him, a bright smile still illuminating her face. The mortification was there, but his reaction made her far less self-conscious.

His white teeth gleamed at her as his smile mirrored her own. He tenderly brushed her hair back from her face and gazed at her with an adoration Haze found unfamiliar. She couldn't remember Mike ever looking at her that way, like she was the human embodiment of Christmas morning happiness. Alfie scooted closer so that the entire length of his body pressed against hers, placing one hand firmly on her ass so that there was no air between their hips. Slowly, his fingertips traced her face and his expression transformed from one of merriment to one of lust. The brown of his eyes darkened, and he leaned forward to kiss her deeply.

Hazel moaned in delight, but broke away from his kiss abruptly. "I'm not sure if I can start this up again," she admitted sheepishly. "Not if my body is gonna make sounds like that."

Alfie smiled as he gently rubbed his nose to hers. "Hey, if you can't laugh with your partner during sex, they aren't the right partner."

She frowned at his explanation. "That goes against everything I know of sex."

"That's because I'm clearly the only one you should be having sex with." He gave her a signature roguish wink and hiked her hip over his to emphasize his point. In one strong thrust, he was sheathed inside her again, twisting to guide Hazel on top.

It was a position she typically avoided because she hated having her body on display so brazenly. However, in the heat of the moment after all Alfie's perfect statements throughout the night, Hazel found a new sense of confidence. She lifted up slightly on her hips to raise her cunt to the tip of his cock before slamming back down. Alfie groaned his approval, reaching up to palm her breasts as she rocked her hips in a circular motion. Hazel threw her head back as the movement created the friction against her clit that she needed. His hips started bucking upwards, matching her rhythm thrust for thrust until her knees quaked at her impending orgasm.

As if sensing that Hazel was at her breaking point, Alfie rolled them so that she was flat on her back while he kneeled at her opening, spreading her legs wide as he used her knees like handlebars. He pounded into her pussy, crying out in a daze as her arousal leaked around his balls. Hazel's eyes rolled back into her head as she had an out of body experience with her climax when he found her G spot and rubbed it like the genie's magic lamp. It only took three more hard thrusts before Alfie joined her over the edge, collapsing down to kiss her deeply once more. The aftershocks left both of them trembling and clinging to one another, the overwhelming sensations leaving them speechless.

Several minutes passed while Hazel tried to control her breathing and the thoughts buzzing around her head. The entire night was completely out of character for her, but she had never had more fun or better sex. Alfie made her want to pivot from The Plan for more than one night. If the orgasm she just had was going to be normal with him, there was no plan on God's green earth that would be worth giving them up. All of her goals for the future dissipated in a plume of smoke as she really considered what a future with Alfie would look like. Clearly, he wasn't a struggling musician, so it was really a matter of merging their schedules. With a frown, she realized most of his gigs would probably be at night, making their schedules polar opposites. And if they couldn't see one another, what would be the point in establishing a relationship?

Her thoughts continued to swirl, ping ponging between all the ways they could make it work and all the reasons why dating Alfie would be a terrible idea. Her eyebrows furrowed in concentration. It was another few minutes before she realized Alfie was staring at her with an amused expression, his smirk back in full force.

"I can literally hear the gears turning in your head," he told her with a grin.

She let out a weak laugh and sighed. "I'm just thinking about what happens now," Hazel admitted with a shrug. All the women's magazine articles taught her that men tended to run for the hills if you brought up any kind of serious commitment too soon, although none of them had prepared her for a night out with a man like Alfie Garza.

He nodded like this was exactly what he expected of her. "Sure, sure," murmured Alfie. "And what conclusion did you draw?"

A flush crept up her neck as a sudden shyness took over. The fear of rejection was trying to dictate her words, but she shoved it down and decided to be honest with him. "That I don't think one night of this will be enough for me," Hazel confessed.

His smile stretched until it dominated his face. He looked more youthful than before, like some of his worries had been lifted by her confession, and the combination with his thick, dark hair and muscular shoulders made Hazel ready for round two. Alfie was breathtaking in a way that shouldn't be legal. But his vulnerability made him that much more real, which was the only reason she hadn't pinched herself yet.

"There was never going to be only one night of this, *aguerrida*," he assured her with a triumphant grin. "I had to make you addicted to me so you'll never leave."

Hazel couldn't help but laugh at him. "This is crazy! People don't just go to parties and instantly start dating someone!"

For a brief moment, Alfie's grin faltered in sadness as he commented, "They do when a sister like Rita plays Santa."

If hearts could burst, Hazel's was on the brink. Grief was such a complicated thing and while she had no doubt that Alfie was happy with her, she knew that he was also holding back the melancholy that can only come from pain. Maybe Rita had paired them together. While she wasn't necessarily religious, Hazel did believe there was *something* after death. Why wouldn't a loving sister want her brother to be happy if that was the case?

"Well, then I hope Rita is sipping margaritas poolside in a fabulous bikini up in Heaven," Hazel offered with a soft smile.

Alfie laughed, shaking his head at the image. "That definitely sounds like her."

"But how is this actually supposed to work, Alfie?" she said. "We have very different schedules and I have all my plans...I'm not dating to date. I am at the point in my life where I want commitment." She fidgeted with her hands, keeping her eyes on her fingers to avoid the uncomfortable tension she felt.

Alfie rolled so that he was full on his stomach, his torso propped up by his elbows, and lifted her chin so that their eyes met. "Hazel, no one can know the future," he explained gently. "Even if I could promise you all of that in this moment, I could have an accident two days from now and never come back." He swallowed audibly, no doubt thinking of how that exact same scenario played out for his sister. "But I can promise you that you've made me feel joy for the first time in months, and that means this is something truly special. The rest we'll just have to figure out as we go."

She shook her head, the protests already on her lips. "No, we have to have a plan!"

"Or what?" Alfie countered, one eyebrow raised in challenge. "Does life stop if you don't have a plan? Do you need a list full of checked boxes at Judgement Day? I thought you knew how to pivot."

She frowned, though she knew his barb was made in jest. "This isn't some corny romcom movie, Alfie," Hazel argued. "I know that my plans are a lot, but there's nothing wrong with wanting things out of life. I have always succeeded in my goals!"

He nodded. "And I'm not saying that you should give them up, or even some horrible cliché about 'living in the moment.' All I'm saying is that we have a spark—a real connection. So let's just see where it leads us, okay?"

Hazel scrubbed her hands over her face in frustration. "And what if it leads us nowhere? I want to be married when I'm thirty, which is next year! And eventually I want to have kids and buy a house in Connecticut, and I just don't want to be one of those women who gives up her life's plan for a good orgasm."

Alfie's face softened and he scooted closer to plant a light kiss on her lips. "We can have as many babies as you want and live anywhere in the world you want someday, *aguerrida*. If I'm a part of your plan, I will make it happen."

Melting. That's what this was.

Hazel's heart was melting.

It was foolish to think she met her Perfect Partner at a random Christmas party in Queens when she was least expecting it, but it was just as foolish to ignore what was developing between them. Alfie said all of the right things with the utmost sincerity. He hadn't made her feel bad about her plans and checklists even when he didn't fully agree with them. And he was right, there was definitely a spark between them. Why shouldn't she see what became of it?

CHAPTER 14

Blair

There should be a monument erected in Mike's name, Blair thought as his mouth performed miracles on her clit. Blair's entire body hummed with pleasure, as if Mike found the secret link to hit all her erogenous zones at once. A carnal fire built within her, the orgasm climbing from the base of her spine. She was going to detonate like a bomb.

"MIKE!" his name burst forth when she came, Christmas lights flickering across her vision. Blair decided then and there to never ask Santa for anything other than Mike's tongue on her clit at all times. That was the best present ever.

He fervently kissed his way up her entire body until he reached her mouth. The taste of her cum on his lips made Blair groan, an opportunity he used to sweep his tongue through her mouth. She loved the way he dominated every inch of her. It was so out of character for the Mike she thought she knew.

Mike leaned down to kiss along her collar bone. His rock hard cock brushed along her abdomen, and Blair wanted to scream in frustration that it couldn't be inside her.

"Have you ever had anal sex before?" Blair panted in his ear.

In an instant, Mike jerked up on both hands to peer at her. His expression was unreadable as he stared. "What did you just say?"

Blair bit her bottom lip in hesitation. Was this too much? Had she pushed him too far? "Never mind. I shouldn't have said anything."

As she turned her face to the side, hoping the sting of rejection wasn't written all over her features, Mike grabbed her firmly by the jaw and forced her to look at him.

"Do I have your permission?" he asked earnestly. His eyebrows rose in excited anticipation.

A grin broke out across her face. "I want to, if you do."

"Merry fucking Christmas!" whispered Mike, more to himself than to her, as he descended on her mouth once more. The kiss only lasted a moment before Mike sat back on his heels, nodding towards his dick. "Get it ready, Blair."

Ooh, Dominant Mike was her new favorite version. Blair never considered herself submissive when it came to sex; it reminded her far too much of how submissive she could be with all the other aspects of her life. But this was different. Blair wanted to submit to Mike, to please him, and in so doing, wanted to signify to him just how arousing she found this side of his personality.

Taking his cock in her mouth, Blair let her saliva pool around him, lubing him up as much as possible. She hadn't had anal sex in a long time, but an instinct told her it would be far more pleasurable with Mike.

"Lay back down," he instructed. His eyes were blown out, pupils dilated so much that the irises were barely visible.

Blair settled onto her back, keeping her feet planted on the floor with her knees bent. What she didn't expect was for Mike to hoist her up by both knees, rocking them to her chest so that her pussy and asshole were bared to him. With a hefty spit, Mike coated her back door with saliva, letting her knees drop so he could use one hand to gently massage the opening.

This wasn't Blair's first backwater rodeo, so she knew the best thing she could do was relax her muscles. Rather than flipping her over as Blair expected, Mike kept her on her back, never losing eye contact as his fingers softly worked her open so he could line the head of his cock at her asshole.

Eye contact made the whole thing more intimate, and rather than remembering her rowdy days as a sorority girl when she first tried anal, Blair focused on the growing feeling between them. This heat, this connection...it felt so *right*. She trusted him implicitly to make this as pleasurable as everything else had been. And Blair wasn't the kind of woman who trusted people easily. There was no way Hazel and Mike ever had this kind of intensity between them. This was solely theirs, a charge that surged as he leaned down on one elbow to place another tender kiss on her lips.

"Are you ready?" he asked.

Blair didn't trust herself to speak, choosing to nod instead. She didn't want to be the only one who voiced the magic brewing between them.

With his gray eyes trained on hers, Blair took a deep breath as his cock slid inside her. Passion blazed in his eyes as if he were awestruck at the privilege she granted him. He hiked one of her knees up higher, giving him more of an angle, and Blair's eyes rolled into the back of her head. It was so tight! She willed her muscles to relax as Mike began to slowly pump.

"Hey!" he barked. "Eyes on me!"

Her eyelids shot open automatically, her body eager to submit to him once more. Mike leaned forward to spear his tongue down her throat. The kiss made her melt, her body going lax with pleasure. His kisses were so dominant, matching the sexy alternate persona he became in this room. She wanted to let him ruin her, claim her, make it impossible for another man to get her off. In just a few short hours, Mike Downey made Blair want an entirely different kind of life.

"Reach down and play with yourself, Blair," Mike commanded. "I want to see you come undone again."

Blair whimpered. Her body already felt like dissolving putty. "I-I don't know if I can do it again."

Mike kissed his way around her jaw, pausing to nibble on her earlobe. "I know you can, baby. Don't make me cum by myself."

His words, caressed so seductively against her skin, sent a second wind through her. Blair slid a hand down between them, using her fingers to rub her clit. Instantly, desire pooled between her legs, her arousal dripping down onto the base of Mike's shaft.

Once her body completely relaxed from her touch, Mike began thrusting harder, her hole no longer fighting the intrusion. Yet another orgasm built at the base of her spine. And since Mike kept his eyes on her face, watching the way her mouth formed the perfect O, Blair finally let herself succumb to the sensation.

She cried out a garbled sound as the orgasm broke free. It was the tipping point for Mike to follow her over the edge, his hips bruising her as he chased his own climax. With a grunt, he gave a last shuddering thrust before collapsing on top of her.

Blair didn't hesitate to wrap both arms and legs around him so that she held him like a koala. She didn't want him to see the tears streaming down her face as the ecstasy of the moment washed over her like a tidal wave. Somehow, the intensity between them only grew as Mike held her back, equally clinging to her as she was to him.

And Blair couldn't help but wonder. Did this night really have to be all there was between them?

CHAPTER 15

Mike

Whoever this dominant alter ego was, Mike never wanted him to leave. Especially if it meant more nights like this with Blair. She was his Christmas miracle and literal dream personified, and it terrified him as much as it thrilled him. There was something almost tangible between them. The closet pulsated with it as if the four walls weren't enough to contain the electricity building.

Mike desperately wanted more of it.

Gently, so as not to hurt her, he withdrew his still semi-hard cock and used one of the tablecloths to wipe it off. Mike folded the tablecloth in half again to find a clean side to wipe along the seam of Blair's entrance, then folded the tablecloth in quarters to clean up her backside. It wasn't much by way of aftercare, but hopefully he could convince Blair to go to his place after this so he could take care of her properly.

And with a jolt, Mike realized that was all he wanted to do. He wanted to take care of Blair at night after they enjoyed more earth-shattering orgasms. He wanted to wake her up with break-fast in bed. He wanted to glance across the room and catch the hint of her smile as she painted at an easel set up by the window. Writing a book would be so much easier with a sexy muse like her before him.

If she wanted to go to Europe, he wanted to go, too. Maybe the sites there would serve as the perfect backdrop for the worlds Mike had to create for his story. All he knew was that he had never been so inspired to write as he was at this very moment, with Blair McAllister in his arms.

But how was he supposed to convey any of this to her? They already agreed it could only be this one night. And ultimately, Mike knew that no matter how strong their feelings might be, Blair would never betray Hazel by being with him. The disappointment of it all almost made him shrivel in despair.

"Blair, I—"

The statement died in his throat when Mike saw Blair was crying.

"Oh my god, did I hurt you?!" he cried, sitting upright to assess her body for damage.

"N-no!" Blair sobbed dramatically. "You're perfect!" With another disparaging wail, she threw an arm over her eyes and let the tears flow, no longer holding back.

Mike's mouth hung open for a moment before he roused himself enough to react. "Blair, talk to me! I don't understand what's happening!" After a quick tug, he pulled her upright, adjusting her so that she sat in his lap, her head tucked under his chin.

She sniffled before responding. "I just don't want this night to end. Even being locked in a closet, this has been the best Christmas party of my life!"

Hope soared from Mike's chest. Having her return his feelings was almost too good to be true.

"Why does it have to end?" he finally settled on asking. It seemed like the best question to ask in case he misread all the signs.

Blair leaned away from him, noisily wiping her nose on her arm. "Because once we leave here, we have to go back to being Mike and Blair!" She said it as if it were obvious, but Mike didn't understand the logic.

"Um..." Statistical analysis, the only skillset he'd ever mastered, didn't really mean much right now because any idiot could tell he had a hundred percent chance of screwing this up. Silence was the best choice until he deciphered what she meant.

"Don't you see?" Blair wailed. "You'll have to go back into hiding because you're Hazel's ex, and I'll have to go back to pretending like I didn't just have the best sex of my life because I'm Hazel's cousin, and then we'll both just be miserably dreaming of what life could have been."

Mike's eyebrows went up as he tried to follow her train of logic. "Or we could just go to Europe together and tell Hazel when the time is right."

Her back went ramrod straight as she drew herself up to her full height and gaped at him. "You want to go to Europe with me?" Blair asked in a daze.

He swallowed thickly, praying for another Christmas miracle that he wasn't that far off the mark. "Yes, I'd love to go to Europe with you. You can learn about art, I can write, and we'll just pick up odd jobs here or there for whatever money we need."

A tense silence hung in the air as Blair blinked at him in disbelief. Then, before Mike had time to react, she launched herself at him, winding both arms around his neck as she laughed in delight.

"This is amazing!" Blair gleamed. "We can do it all together! And then maybe you'll find the inspiration for your book, and I'll finally paint again, and it will just be the most perfect year—"

Her enthusiasm was too much. Mike just had to kiss her again. Plus, it was unlikely that she could calm down enough to resume normal conversation. If her voice got any higher, only dogs would hear.

"Let's do it," Mike agreed. "Let's go to Europe together."

Blair frowned for a moment. "And what about Hazel?"

A twinge of guilt nagged at him, but Mike found himself far more concerned for Blair's welfare than anything else. "When you're ready, we'll tell her together. She loves you and she'll want you to be happy, Blair."

Although she nodded, Mike could tell she wasn't entirely convinced. Then again, neither was he.

"If only Hazel could have her own Christmas miracle," he joked. "Maybe Santa left her a new boyfriend under the tree."

Blair rolled her eyes before she began pulling her clothes back on. "Yeah, maybe she actually went home with that hot guy talking to her outside the bathroom."

If nothing else, this right here proved just how far gone Mike was. For the first time since their breakup, the thought of Hazel finding someone new brought him intense joy. He meant what he said earlier; Hazel truly was one of a kind. She just wasn't right for him. If there was a man out there who could check off all Hazel's boxes and make her happy, Mike wanted that for her.

"It's the most wonderful time of the year," Mike reminded her. "Anything is possible."

CHAPTER 16

Alfie

Alfie wondered if there was a story somewhere that explained how Cupid worked hand in hand with Saint Nick because he was clearly lovestruck. Everything about Hazel drew him in, from the way her nose crinkled as she concentrated, to the lilting quality of her laugh, all the way down to how her toes curled when she came. It was the toe-curling feature Alfie intended to become highly acquainted with, as he suckled on her clit to draw out yet another orgasm.

Hazel moaned, her hips grinding into his mattress. If he had his way, Alfie would keep her chained to it because it was definitely where she belonged.

"I'm spent!" she cried, her body going limp. The grin she sent his way made Alfie's heart stop. Hazel was so beautiful. He loved the way her hair fanned out on the pillows, the twinkle in her eyes as she gazed at him, and the way she seemed to be more and more at ease with him as the night went on.

They were nearing dawn, having spent the majority of the night wrapped up in exploring each other's bodies. True to his word, Alfie tried to lick, kiss, and worship every inch of skin, certain that each new angle was actually her best one. When they stopped for a late night snack break that resulted in Hazel wearing whipped cream that Alfie cleaned off her with his tongue, he pulled her into the shower with him.

Hazel replied in kind, by dropping to her knees right there on the tile and gifting his cock with a blowjob that practically drained him dry. The sight of her at his feet, with her cheeks hollowed out to accommodate his girth, wet hair plastered down the sides of her face led Alfie to one solitary conclusion: Hazel McAllister had to agree to be his before she could leave his townhouse.

Now, his heart threatened to burst as she snuggled into the center of his bed, getting comfortable and pulling the covers up. Hazel folded down the blanket to pat the space beside her. Alfie wasted no time crawling in next to her, sighing in relief when she nuzzled into his chest and wound one of her legs between his. Her eyelids fluttered closed, and even as she drifted off into sleep, the smile remained on her lips.

For someone who needed to be in control as much as Hazel seemed to, the fact that she trusted him enough to fall asleep on him was not lost on Alfie. This was a gift, one he had no intention of losing.

Wrapping both arms around her, Alfie whispered into her hair, "Hazel? Do you believe things happen for a reason?"

"Yep," she sighed, on the verge of sleep.

"I do, too. I think Rita sent you to me so that I wouldn't be alone for Christmas."

Suddenly wide awake, Hazel's eyes darted to his as she rested her chin on his chest.

And despite her intense focus, Alfie realized there was no

longer any apprehension in her eyes. Hazel wasn't scared of what he said. The realization made him bolder, hardly daring to believe how quickly and how far he was willing to push this.

"In fact, I think she sent you to me so that I wouldn't be alone at all," he admitted.

"What are you saying?" Hazel asked hesitantly.

Alfie grinned. "I'm saying, I want this, *aguerrida*. However you need to label it, I am all in."

"Just like that?" Hazel raised an eyebrow as she surveyed his face carefully.

She could look at it all day. There would be nothing but sincerity.

"Yes," Alfie replied simply. "I'm a man who gets what he wants. And I want you. Preferably naked in my bed like this every night, but I suppose I'll let you get dressed so I can take you out and show you off sometimes, too."

Hazel snorted as she rolled her eyes. "Oh, is that right? How gracious of you!"

Alfie smiled, loving the way the breath caught in her throat from the sight.

"And what about what I want?" she challenged. "Don't I get a say in this?"

"Baby, you get to call the shots. Whatever you want, however you want it, I'll make happen. I just won't share you, so don't ever ask." Just the thought of Hazel with another man was enough to drive Alfie unhinged. "Violence" wouldn't cover the level of carnage he would unleash.

With a satisfying sigh, Hazel settled back down against his chest. "I am not the kind of woman who can practice polyamory, thank you! Besides, you're enough to keep any woman on her toes!"

"Oh, I'll keep you on your toes!" Alfie agreed. "But only so I can drive my dick in harder."

He didn't need to see her face to know that she rolled her eyes again and blushed.

After a long pause, enough time to where Alfie assumed she finally fell asleep, Hazel whispered. "Okay. I'm in."

"Yeah?!" Alfie sat up, forcing Hazel to sit up, too. A triumphant grin stretched across his face. This was better than any Christmas present he ever received as a child.

"I can't promise you that I won't have more checklists," Hazel confessed shyly. "And I'll need to pivot to a new plan. Your job is a little unpredictable."

Now it was Alfie's turn to roll his eyes. "I think you mean 'flexible.' As in, whenever you start popping out all those babies you want us to have, I can stay home with them so you can keep being super woman at your job. Or we can just live off my royalties. I don't really care either way. Finances can be up to you." Alfie shrugged.

Hazel adjusted herself so that she sat cross-legged. "What do you mean?"

It wasn't meant to sound arrogant, so Alfie tried to add a little humility to his tone as he explained, "The royalties from my songs. I wrote two songs for a couple of my mom's movies a while back, and they were both number one hits in Spain. I normally earn around two million a year for each. Then there's my trust fund that I haven't touched, and some other investments my family made on my behalf."

If he wasn't so fearful of her rejection, Alfie would find the way her mouth opened and closed like a goldfish to be funny. Whatever answer Hazel expected, it was obviously nothing like what he actually said.

"Is that a problem?" Alfie asked. This wouldn't be the first time a relationship went off the rails because of his famous family, and he found himself waiting with bated breath for her to respond.

Hazel leaned forward, planting a teasing kiss on his lips. "You mean I get to date a sexy, talented millionaire *and* he'll put up with my neuroses? You drive a hard bargain, Alfie Garza." She kissed him again. This time the kiss lasted longer, raising his blood pressure and his erection so that it tented the covers.

"Merry Christmas, *aguerrida*," Alfie whispered, grabbing onto both of Hazel's hips and yanking her onto his lap. As a testament to how much Hazel already accepted him and the intent behind his words, she lifted up and sank down onto his cock, both of them groaning in delight.

"Hazel, I don't have a condom on," Alfie pointed out.

She rolled her hips, effectively erasing any other argument he could possibly articulate. "I'm on birth control," Hazel assured him. "You get this one time as your Christmas gift and then we're keeping it wrapped until the wedding night."

"*Gracias a los dioses!*" Alfie growled. *Thank the gods!* "How did Santa know exactly what I wanted?"

Hazel leaned forward, bracing her arms on the headboard so that her glorious tits hung in his face. "Just a lucky guess!"

Alfie's mouth latched onto one of her nipples, the resulting whimpers urging him to continue. He hung back, content to let her take the lead and feel in control for once. There wouldn't be many opportunities for her to do that in their bedroom. Alfie had to make sure she remained satiated and happy.

As he felt her pussy walls clamp down as another orgasm wracked through her, Alfie rose up to kiss her fiercely, following her with his own release. He had no idea how he even found the strength to come after how much sex they'd already had, but then again, as he felt her luscious curves against his skin, Alfie could already feel the need for her returning. He literally could not get enough of her.

Hazel giggled as she dropped back down on the mattress beside him. A faint light just barely crept in through the windows. Morning had arrived, and Alfie couldn't remember how long it had been since he felt glad to see it. Certainly not since Rita's passing.

"Shit! Shit! Shit!" The words came out all in one breath. His girlfriend leapt out of bed, canvassing the floor for her discarded clothes.

His girlfriend. Alfie loved how that phrase sounded in his head when in reference to her.

Although he didn't love the speed in which she dressed and dashed out of his room.

"Hey, wait a minute!" Alfie called, following her out the door and down the stairs. Hazel shoved a boot on while trying to simultaneously push an arm through the sleeve of her coat. "Where are you going?"

"I never heard back from Blair!" Hazel shrieked. "What if she's dead in a ditch somewhere?!"

Alfie had to bite down on his lip to keep from laughing. Anxiety was real, he knew that, but damn it, did Hazel have to look so adorable when she had a panic attack?

"She probably just crashed at Dustin's," he offered. "I know people do that at his place all the time." His neighbor threw ridiculous parties every weekend when he pretended to be a DJ. Alfie knew for a fact that Dustin just created playlists on his computer because he helped Dustin find new songs every once in a while. Dustin thought being a DJ would get him laid, despite all evidence to the contrary.

"Really?" Hazel's face lit up with hope, which Alfie found as attractive as her panic.

"Yeah. Just let me throw on some clothes and I'll go over there with you. I know where he keeps the spare key."

"Thank you! Thank you!" Hazel practically danced on the balls of her feet, throwing her arms around Alfie in her relief.

He gripped her tightly. All he wanted was for Hazel to keep turning to him in moments like these. She could be as anxious as she needed because Alfie would be her rock.

"You don't have to thank me, baby," he reminded her. "This is what boyfriends do."

At this acknowledgement, Hazel visibly relaxed, her shoulders sinking and her posture becoming more natural. If Alfie had to guess, there was still a small part of her brain that continued to doubt him. But that was okay because it meant Alfie just needed to keep her coming in his bed every night and showering her with praise and compliments all day long.

Santa really outdid himself this year. Hazel McAllister made up for every past, present, and future Christmas. Alfie would never ask for anything else again.

CHAPTER 17

Hazel

A hundred different scenarios played out in Hazel's mind, no matter how much Alfie assured her that Blair was fine. Her cousin couldn't be fine because she never answered any of Hazel's messages. It was a move so unlike Blair that Hazel frantically started to dial 911 before Alfie snatched the phone from her hand.

"Let's just pop over to Dustin's and see what he says."

Alfie expertly located a fake rock at the base of his neighbor's stairs and pulled out the spare key. As soon as he let them inside, Hazel gasped triumphantly.

"Ah ha!" she cried. "That's Blair's purse and coat!" She pointed to a leather satchel covered in paint splatter and a bright red wool coat trimmed in white fur still lying on the stairs.

"Blair really gets into the holiday spirit, doesn't she?" Alfie commented playfully.

Hazel sighed in exasperation. "That's not helpful! Where could she be?"

Empty Solo cups and drink bottles littered the floor. Two

people she didn't recognize took up the couch, while a third person lay curled in the fetal position under the coffee table. Holiday music still blared from the speakers, but with a click of a button, Alfie turned them off.

"Maybe she's back in the den!" Hazel suggested. She rushed around the corner, kicking more discarded cups, bottles, and plates along the way. Although she paused to glance in the kitchen, there was nothing in it other than more trash on every surface.

"Blair!" she called as she entered the den. The back door was still open, and now that the room had emptied of writhing bodies, the air felt frigid. Her breath came out in white puffs. More strangers sprawled on the couch and floor, but none of them sported the blue-streaked curls of her cousin.

"Could she be upstairs?!" Hazel panicked. True fear laced through her veins. Maybe she needed to tackle Alfie and get her phone back. Hazel raced back down the hallway, outright screaming her cousin's name. She no longer cared if she woke anybody up. As far as Hazel was concerned, every person in the townhouse was Suspect Number One.

Pounding echoed from a door to her right, just before Hazel reached Alfie in the living room. He obviously heard it, too, meaning it wasn't her anxiety getting the best of her as he pulled Hazel behind him to assess the door. With a lingering glance over his shoulder, Alfie yanked hard on the handle...

Causing Blair and Mike Downey to fall out on the floor at their feet!

"Blair! Mike!" Hazel's voice reached new decibels as she stared down at them in shock.

"Woah, it reeks of sex in there!" Alfie waved a hand in front of his face, grimacing at the smell, as he shoved the door closed.

It smells like sex? What?

Hazel must've been hallucinating because she couldn't imagine a world where her best friend and cousin would hook up with her ex-boyfriend, the man who broke her heart. They didn't even like each other!

Although, as Hazel glanced over at Alfie, who helped Blair to her feet, she had to admit that Mike didn't really break her heart. More like bruised her ego by disrupting her five year plan. And it turned out, The Perfect Partner just might defy her checklist anyway.

"Blair, what is going on?" Hazel asked.

Her cousin had the good grace to look sheepish, keeping her eyes downcast as she fidgeted with the hem of the oversized t-shirt she wore. Mike wouldn't make eye contact with her either. Instead, he tried to wrap an arm around Blair, only for her cousin to push his hand away with a tiny shake of her head.

Nobody said anything for a moment, the air charged with tension. It was Alfie who broke it by holding out his hand to Mike. "Hi, I'm Alfie Garza," he introduced himself. "Hazel's boyfriend." He beamed as he said it, and Hazel couldn't help the way her heart fluttered at hearing the declaration out loud. She was practically giddy with excitement just to know that Alfie was hers.

To her surprise, both Mike and Blair's heads popped up, equally as enthusiastic at Alfie's announcement.

"Not bad, Hazel!" Blair said appraisingly.

Hazel blushed. "It's a recent development."

"I'll say!" Blair replied. "Good for you. You're happy, right? Filled with that Christmas spirit and this stud muffin's sperm?"

Alfie threw back his head and laughed loud enough for the people behind him to jerk awake. "Oh, I like her!"

Hazel closed her eyes and counted to ten, silently praying for the floor to open up and swallow her whole. "Yes, Blair, I'm very happy. Can you please stop acting so cagey and tell me what's going on? Why were you in there with Mike?"

"We got locked in," Mike explained apologetically. His eyes were kind, not showing a hint of jealousy or hurt that Hazel had moved on. "There's no door handle on the inside."

Alfie nodded. "Yeah, there's a door handle at the bottom. You just have to press down with your shoe."

"WHAT?!" Blair and Mike yelled in unison.

"Yeah, see?" Alfie opened the door and pointed towards a small crevice at the bottom, just big enough for the toes of a human foot. "It's supposed to be helpful so that anyone carrying boxes out can open the door without setting anything down. I have a closet just like it at my place next door."

Mike and Blair exchanged an incredulous look that Hazel did not miss.

"Now, if you don't mind, I'm gonna close this again," Alfie said awkwardly. "It really does smell...ripe...in there." He winced slightly, probably hoping his words didn't sound offensive to her cousin.

"Blair?" Hazel gazed pointedly at her, determined to get a real answer out.

Blair's eyes went wide before she crumbled onto Hazel's chest like a toddler. "We did it, okay?! Mike and I screwed around all night long while we were locked in that closet together! And it was amazing, and *he* was amazing, and now I'm really happy because he's going to go on my European trip, too!"

Sniffles echoed loudly under Hazel's chin as Blair clung to her. Mike, to his credit, kept his head held high, an unencumbered hope lining his features.

"We don't want to hurt you, Hazel," Mike insisted, "but everything Blair said is true. I know it sounds crazy, but it's like we had a Christmas miracle or something. I really care about her." He nodded towards Blair, whose cries had somewhat muffled.

Hazel searched her feelings, waiting for something akin to anger or betrayal to emerge. Yet there wasn't even a tinge of sadness or grief. One glance to her left showed her hunky new Spanish boyfriend who already wanted to be a part of all her future plans. Like Alfie said earlier, everything happened for a reason. Maybe there was a reason for the entire night, a Christmas party gone awry to help the right people find each other.

After a pregnant pause, Hazel asked, "Where all in Europe are you going?"

Blair tearfully pulled away. Her mouth fell open, and she gazed at Hazel in alarm. "You're not mad?"

The pitiful hope in her voice knocked some sense into Hazel. No matter what, all she wanted was for her cousin to be happy. While it was a little weird to think Blair might be happy with Mike, of all people, in an odd sort of way, it made sense. Mike had a lot of the same qualities as Blair, which was probably one of the things that drew Hazel to him when they first met. No matter how strange it might feel however, Blair obviously wanted Hazel's approval on this, and she refused to be another person who let her down.

"Of course not, Blair Bear!" Hazel gushed. "All I care about is your happiness. And I know for a fact that Mike is one of the good ones."

She pulled her cousin into a fierce hug, both women now

with tears in their eyes. Hazel could see Mike and Alfie both smiling at them.

"So!" Alfie clapped his hands together gleefully. "Who's hungry? I know a great breakfast place nearby!"

"We are STARVING!" Blair cried. She grabbed Mike's hand, smiling up at him in a way that made Hazel's heart soar. It had been years since Blair looked so happy.

That alone solidified Hazel's decision. She stepped into Alfie's waiting arms, blushing as he gently kissed her forehead. "C'mon, guys, let's call an Uber!"

Mike and Blair both groaned. "Can't we just take the train?" Mike grumbled.

"It's so much cheaper," Blair added.

Alfie's eyebrows rose hopefully as he watched Hazel's face. "It's time to break the cycle, *aguerrida*. I promise, this won't hurt."

Even Hazel could admit when she was outnumbered. "Fine! But that means breakfast is on Alfie!" Her eyes danced with mirth as she winked at her boyfriend before leading the group out the door.

Mike paused to help Blair into her coat before donning his own. Hazel and Alfie waited, arm in arm, on the sidewalk for their friends to join them. They kept up an animated chatter about Europe and the grand adventure Blair planned all the way to the subway entrance.

They were roughly halfway there when heavy snowflakes began to fall. Hazel had a newfound appreciation for the way the snow gathered around all the Christmas decorations lining the block.

"What has you grinning?" Alfie whispered conspiratorially.

Hazel shrugged. "Just wondering how Santa is gonna top this next year."

About the Author

Samantha Gail is a former Probation Parole Officer who supervised sex offenders before deciding she needed something with happily ever afters. Her work falls into multiple genres, primarily thriller, romance, and fantasy. She currently manages a bookstore and writes when she's not spending time with her three children and three fur babies.

Samantha loves to connect with readers and watches her Instagram DM's like a hawk! Don't hesitate to reach out with questions, reviews, and requests.

Also by Samantha Gail

Epoch

Full Circle

Behind My Hazel Eyes